Homesteading the Land

Phelps Mill – 1890

*Written and illustrated
by Jan Smith*

Book 1

**… a look at the daily life of a
homesteading family of five's
survival in the year 1890 as they
adjust to prairie schooner travel,
sod house living, log cabin life and
the clearing of land …**

Acknowledgements

Writing any lengthy piece is rarely one person's final product. I have many to thank for providing material and encouragement along the way.

First, my friendship with Rich Osman, whose historical background and interest in Phelps Mill, enabled me to *see* through his eyes and read through his personal collection of data about the mill. What a boon!

Second, the Otter Tail County Historical Society's collection of Fergus Falls newspapers became the chronological factual material for the basis of the story line, including ideas for some of the sketches.

Last, my love goes to my husband, Bruce, who always encouraged, never doubted that the project would come to fruition. His continuous reading and re-reading for clarity and content guided me along the way more than anyone.

Blessings to each of you.

The most salient facts, events and circumstances set forth in this book are the events related to Maine (Phelps Mill), 1890. These events are recounted truthfully from records found at the Historical Society, Fergus Falls, Minnesota, while browsing the archives on microfiche to the limits of the author's perception and ability. Elaborations to enhance readability do not compromise any main truth.

Many of the persons in this book are identified by their true names. All other characters are fictional and were given fictitious names.

This work is historical fiction, enhanced by the actual events so documented in the *Fergus Falls Journal Weekly*, 1890, reported primarily in the "Maine News."

E-Book version of **Rambling 'Round Maine**

A. THOMAS MILL
B. THOMAS SOD HOUSE
C. THOMAS HOUSE
D. THOMAS BARN
E. ROOST
F. CHEESE
   HOUSE

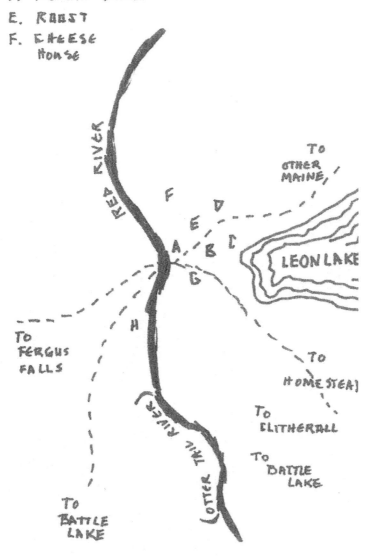

G. McConkey's Store   H. CHEESE STORE

Chapter

1

"Home" as We Travel

Living in the soddy (sod house) was heaven compared to where we first lived when we came to the Maine (Phelps) area. The family arrived here on Murphy's fifth birthday. Our first "home" on the land that Dad bought was a tent much like the tents that John the Baptist made and sold in the Bible. Grandpa and Grandma used that same tent when they came West with the Prairie Schooner. Dad and John Barry, our neighbor who owns the land to the east of us, got the soddy built. Mr. Barry comes from a big family so we had a lot of help from his six boys and him, hauling the sod sections and putting up the walls and roof. I was only eleven but I was the "go fer," fetching for them what I could. But I am ahead of my story . . .

Traveling up to this area from Grandpa John's was slow. We used the same prairie schooner that brought Grandpa and Grandma West. Dad bought a team of good sturdy Belgian workhorses which pulled our covered wagon full of all our belongings. Those Belgians are a matched pair! I didn't know what that meant until I saw them pull the schooner. Dad hardly has to tell them what to do; they seem to know which one is to turn and pull whatever way. Once I thought I'd help Dad out one morning on the trail. I got them harnessed up. It was a struggle for me. The hames and straps are so heavy for those big horses, so much so that I could hardly lift the harnesses to get them on each horse. I wondered why the two horses fussed for me. I have driven them behind the schooner when Mom and Nise (our nickname for my sister) have been busy, handling the reins without any difficulty. Usually they just stand and wait for the harness' hook up. Turned out I had the two hooked up wrong! When Dad put the one horse on the opposite side of the other and re-hooked the harness, they were just fine! One is used to being on the left and the other is used to being on the right. From then on I called them Lefty and Lena.

Dad also bought another smaller horse, used to a saddle and also used to pulling a one horse cart. Murphy named him Benji. Grandpa will bring up the cutter one day soon when he comes to help build the barn and house. We will use this paint horse, Benji, and cutter, or two-wheeled cart, to get to school, and to visit the neighbors and neighboring towns for supplies. Dad brought along a brindled cow that recently freshened, a heifer he had bred just before we came on the trail, and two young ewes that will lamb in the spring so Mom will have wool to card for clothes she will knit.

We moved slower for the animals as we headed up the trail. Dad told us that it was better to take our time, so that the animals would stay healthy. Faster travel could injure them and we couldn't afford to lose any of them.

It was my responsibility to keep the two ewes on the trail. They were two independent sorts, more interested in eating than staying on the trail. One day the one ewe wandered off ahead and started bleating loudly! I had been shooting at squirrels, hoping to get two or three for the stew pot for supper and wasn't paying too good attention to the ewes. I ran to see where the bleating came from and found the ewe had fallen in a small ravine. She was stuck feet up in some branches that had lodged into the cavern made by heavy rains. No wonder she was hollering! I'd holler too if I were hanging upside down.

It was lunch time so we stopped here and Mom got lunch ready while Dad and I got the ewe out. That wasn't easy. Dad had to crawl down into the side of the ravine to get under the branch and push it up so I could grab the ewe. It's a good thing she didn't weigh much yet. She was scared and kicked pretty hard. I finally got a hold on the two back legs and gave a yank. Out she came kicking me in the forehead as I pulled her out. I gave a yell and she cut loose with another kick and ran to her pal, the other ewe, hollering some more! I hope she told the other ewe not to be so stupid. Dad sure told me to pay better attention. When he realized I was looking for some meat for supper, he mellowed some. Mom patched me up as best she could. The bleeding from the slice the hoof made in my forehead stopped eventually. I have a scar from the kick.

Some livestock that we want we did not try to herd with us. Dad knows a fellow in the area where we are going that raises and sells pigs, so he will buy two when we get the pigpen ready. He intends to feed them a few boiled potatoes once a day and let them root in the pen for the rest. Pigs love acorns which we will gather, fattening fairly well when they eat them. Dad will let them fatten like that until he is able to feed them mainly the grain we will raise. He will have to plan to sow five acres of oats for every three pigs he has. Dad is able to broadcast 1 ½ bushels of seed to each acre, so he will need the 7 ½ bushels he brought with in the schooner, just to grow enough oats for the three pigs he will buy. If we cut some weeds for them now and then and feed them rotten potatoes, we will be all right. Dad thinks he will average about 30 bushels of oats to the acre, so he plans on buying more pigs after the first harvest. If we can get the sows bred, they can have seven or more pigs. If that happens, Dad will not have to buy any more pigs.

Chickens are another matter. We know that Mom needs chickens for the eggs for baking and cooking other food. Dad plans to have the stage bring six "cluckers" and a rooster from Fergus Falls, a neighboring town to the west, once we get settled. I have been on the watch for guinea hens and their nests along the trail. Whenever I spy one that has eggs in the nest, I take one or two if the hen is sitting on a group. Mom has used these instead of chicken eggs for cooking when she has no other eggs. They are smaller but still are eggs and can be used like all other eggs for cooking.

Our travels up the road caused quite a stir as we came by other homesteads. Some thought we were crazy herding all the livestock with us. Others were envious, wishing they had some of our animals on their homestead. Dad was determined that we would be comfortable and have most of what we needed to get settled that first year. Not knowing what was available, Dad and Mom brought much of what they thought we would need with us.

For the most part, people along the way were very generous. Most had been on the trail sometime themselves and had others help them, so they helped us as much as they could. Some fed us lunch or supper as we came by. Others even invited us to sleep in their spare room. Some offered a barn stall to bed down in. We were particularly grateful for a stall in a barn one night when it was really storming. We all were pretty wet from the rain that night, keeping the animals in tow. None of us felt like crawling into the schooner to sleep as wet as we were, so we were very thankful for the offer of a barn. Dad pulled the schooner alongside the barn and we got settled in the two empty stalls. We put the animals in a pen outside so

8

they wouldn't wander off. Once we had eaten the bread and stew that the wife brought us, we got out of our wet clothes, hung them on the rafters to dry and lay down in the straw with one of Mom's quilts as cover.

It was hard to get up the next morning. None of us had been so comfortable in a long while. Sleeping in the straw in the barn stall was much better than trying to find room in the schooner. Usually, Dad and I take a bed roll and put it under the schooner at night, sort of sleeping under the stars but protected overhead by the bed of the schooner. Dad always has his gun by his side and loaded as we lay there under the wagon bed whenever we sleep outside like that in case there is trouble. After we got reloaded and were leaving in the morning, Mom gave the lady two pair of mittens she had knit along the way as a thank you for their sharing of food and hospitality. Likewise, she sent us on our way with fresh bread.

Chapter

2

Grandpa's Stories

We came up from Southern Minnesota, where my grandparents homesteaded in 1865. Grandpa John paid $125.00 for the schooner. Grandpa spent a lot of money for the schooner, but it is built very well. It has a double box with end gates and rods and a seat in the front. When it was nice, we'd open the canvas and let the air blow through. That seems years ago even if I am only eleven now.

It was fun to listen to Grandpa and Grandma as they told us about their trips across the ocean in the early '60's. Grandma came a year earlier than Grandpa. Mom, Nise, Murphy and I (Dad calls me Nivek most of the time) stayed with them while Dad went North to find homestead land. Grandpa came over on the *Ocean Queen* across the Atlantic. The *Queen* was an iron-screw steamer 137 feet long and 18 feet wide. That doesn't seem very big to me. When it was at full steam, Grandpa said it traveled at 50 horsepower. When Grandpa came over, the ship was packed with 150 passengers and 75 crew members. He felt like a sardine.

This trip was a maiden voyage for the *Queen*, crossing the Atlantic. Her usual route was traveling between Hull and Rotterdam. Its owner, a Mr. Tyne, wanted to see the "New World" and decided to make one trip with her across the ocean. The trip was so successful that Mr. Tyne continued making monthly journeys. Grandpa said she had tall masts that held sails which helped push the ship forward when the wind was strong enough. It took 15 days to cross the ocean. Food was good and plentiful for those who could eat. Many passengers were seasick the entire trip across. After the first three days at sea and so many passengers sick, the smells below where everybody slept were horrible. Some passengers came into the New York harbor so weak they could hardly walk off the gangplank to shore. Grandpa had worked for a time on the fishing boats as a cook in Norway and was used to the rocking of a boat; so he spent time on deck, watching the men working the sails of the ship, to stay out of the hold where so many were sick. This way he stayed in the fresh air and was able to avoid most of the bad smells.

Grandpa soon learned that crossing the ocean on the ship was easy for him. Getting through immigration took time. The lines were long and people were cranky because most did not feel well or speak the new world language. Grandpa was lucky, thankful that he had learned English from my great grandma Marie who was a school teacher in Norway. She had somehow learned to speak the American language and made sure her five kids learned it too.

As Grandpa got closer to the registration line, he realized that his name would cause problems. When it was his turn and the immigration officer asked Grandpa for his name, Grandpa said, "Gittle (pronounced yet-la) Johan (yo han) Stromstad." This didn't sound American enough for the officer, so the officer Americanized the name. For the rest of Grandpa's life, he became John G. Stromstad. In some ways, Grandpa was glad. He was tired of being teased about his name.

Grandpa told us one night before we left to come here how he made his way west once he left New York and traveled to Chicago where he met Grandma. Once he got through immigration, he found out where the train station was. He had been to Oslo many times so he was familiar with a big city, but he did not realize how difficult New York would be. So many people did not speak the English language as he learned it or Norwegian. Grandpa was very glad he paid attention in school and learned how to read English too. He read the signs and finally found the train station.

When Grandpa got inside the station, about ready to buy his ticket, he spied a "Help Wanted" poster, advertising for a boiler man. He asked at the ticket window about the job and was sent to another office. The engineer on the train was in the office, also Norwegian, and hired Grandpa on the spot. The boiler man job was easy for Grandpa. Most of the time, Grandpa sat and watched the gauge on the box. If the temperature gauge got too low, he would throw more wood in the firebox. Much of the time, he was able to watch the scenery as the train traveled down the track.

When the train neared Chicago, Grandpa told the engineer that he was getting off and wondered if he could get his pay, which was a dollar a day. The engineer was sad to see him leave and told Grandpa that if he ever wanted to work and ride for free somewhere again, Grandpa was supposed to "look up" the engineer. After

Grandpa reloaded the wood box for the continued trip once the train had stopped in Chicago, the engineer paid Grandpa and wished him well in America.

Once off the train, Grandpa walked "up town" and saw a sign for a short order cook. With his letter in hand from his boss in Norway where he worked, Grandpa walked in and asked about the job. He was hired and put to work immediately. When his shift was done for the night, Grandpa asked where he could find a room. He was told of a rooming house around the corner from the café. Off he went, found the rooming house and got a room from a lady working behind the desk. That "lady" was Grandma, the lady Grandpa married a year later and brought by schooner to Southern Minnesota.

Grandma was Norwegian too and had been here two years already, so the two of them spent many hours talking about the "Old Country" when they were not working. During this time, people of the same country background tended to stick together. In the big cities like New York and Chicago, there were neighborhoods of Norwegians, Swedes, Poles, etc. Many of those people eventually moved West in search of land much like Grandpa and Grandma did. Sometimes whole towns along the way would spring up that were a group of these same nationality people. Grandpa told me that sometimes in those areas American English became a second language because most people in the towns preferred to speak the "mother tongue."

More than once Grandpa told us a story about himself when he was younger. Grandpa was educated for the time and a smart man. He had gotten his high school diploma. In Chicago when it was slow in the café, he would read the daily newspaper. This is where Grandpa saw the advertisement for homestead land in Minnesota. As he and Grandma came West, he bartered for (or bought if he had the money) books, magazines and newspapers. Grandpa loved poetry and often wrote poems for us when he wasn't busy reading something else.   That must be where I got my love for reading.   While we were there, he helped us learn as much as we could about the history of America, especially of Minnesota and the area around here.

Some of the most memorable stories Grandpa told came from the personal stories of his neighbors. Minnesota was a wild land to settle in the 1860's when he and Grandma came West into Southern Minnesota.   The Sioux Indian uprising took place during this time.   Battles that included hangings and scalpings were very bloody. Once the battle was over, a truce of sorts between the Indians and the Whites lasted for some time.   Some of Grandpa' and Grandma's neighbors were killed during this uprising.

Sometimes I don't blame the Sioux for fighting. Food was short because disease, a blight, ruined the crops.   The Indians began to forage for what food they could find to feed their families.   Promised money from the government did not come so they could not buy food.   In desperation, one Indian foraging party attacked a settler family near Acton.   Soon after, the tribal members convinced Little Crow to declare war against the settlers. A Dakota force attacked the Lower Sioux Agency.   Most of the people living at the Agency and most of the troops at Fort Ridgely were killed.   Most of the town of New Ulm, Minnesota, was burned.   Many Indians and settlers were killed during this time.   Grandpa said that this battle included the worst Indian hangings our country has ever seen.   Sometimes even today an occasional small Indian band will still cause trouble, so Grandpa says there remains a lot of mistrust between the Indians and the Whites in this area.   Grandpa has never had any trouble with the Indians that travel through.   In fact, Grandpa trades with them for herbs and medicines made by their Medicine Man.

Another of Grandpa's neighbors, Jim Spielmann who has parents who still live in Germany, served in the Minnesota Regiment during the Civil War. Jim was a member of the First Minnesota who became heroes during the Battle of Gettysburg. He is one of the few left to tell the story of the fighting during these battles. Grandpa told us that in July of 1863 the fighting shifted back and forth between the North and the South. Sometimes the North seemed to be winning. At other times it was the South. On June 29th, the First Minnesota made a forced march of 33 miles to reach the battlefield. I wanted to ask Grandpa if they walked that far in one day, but he was so wound up in his storytelling that I couldn't get his attention. Some of this group, or regiment as Grandpa called them that were assigned to this unit, were gone on other duties. There were only 262 men available under the command of Colonel William Colvill, waiting for orders to fight. Two riders on horseback came in to camp and the troops in camp were ordered to take up their fighting positions on high ground just to the north of camp.

The rider said that Confederate forces under the command of Longstreet and Hill were moving forward, firing hard on the Union troops close to the Minnesota unit's field position. The Union troops began to retreat past the spot where the First Minnesota Regiment was lined up. Union General Hancock felt that the Confederate rush must be stopped until reinforcements could arrive. Hancock galloped up to Colonel Colvill and gave the order to "charge their lines."

Jim told Grandpa that every man in the Minnesota Regiment knew that to charge the Confederate forces was almost certain death. Their thin line of men was only one hundred yards long and had to go across an open field and up a hill. An order was an order, so the troops did what they were told to do. Without hesitation, the First Minnesota furiously charged the much larger number of Confederate soldiers. The Confederates did not expect so

15

small a group to charge and in confusion fell back in disorder. Minutes dragged out and finally the Union reinforcements arrived to help the Minnesota Regiment and the danger was ended. Only 47 were left in the Regiment when the battle was done.

After the battle, General Hancock explained his orders. Hancock had been told there were reinforcements coming up the road and needed to gain five minutes time. Hancock also felt that the Confederates forward movement needed to be stopped. Hancock knew he was sending most of this unit to its death by his order. He was so very proud of the bravery of the Minnesota group that willingly made the charge. So many men died that day in order to gain five minutes time so that the reinforcements could arrive which stopped the Confederate advance in its tracks and changed the outcome of the entire Civil War.

Mom was very uneasy when Grandpa was retelling Jim's story of the battle. She was afraid that we kids would have nightmares from picturing in our minds the wounds suffered by Jim and the deaths of his friends and fellow troops. Mom wished Grandpa would have talked more about the *glory* of the war and *reason* behind the fighting, not just the fighting. Whenever I see Jim, I always go up and hug him. The heavy fire that his unit faced along with all the bloody memories often bothers Jim, especially at night. To this day, Jim has nightmares of the death and the destruction that surrounded him that day. Grandpa is one of the few people that Jim talks to willingly about his war experiences. Grandpa has always been a good listener, even for me when I have troubles.

Chapter

3

Building the Soddy

One day as we were traveling up a trail on the other side of Battle Lake, Dad told us to get ready because we were soon "home." Murphy, Nise and I couldn't believe that our journey was to end. It took a little longer than Dad thought because the recent rains had filled the sloughs and flooded some of the roads between the sloughs and lakes enough that we had to be careful not to mire down the heavily loaded schooner.

Seeing the building of Mr. Thomas' mill and Mr. McConkey's store in Maine (Phelps Mill) for the first time put smiles on all our faces. Getting to the spot where Dad planned to build the soddy, and eventually our log house made Mom cry with joy, knowing the worst of the move was over. It was late when we got to *our place* so that night we slept as we always did - in the schooner and under it, knowing in the next days we would pitch the tent Grandpa John sent with us, beginning the sod house as soon as we could.

Putting the tent up was easy. Many of the new neighbors, including Mr. and Mrs. Barry and their six boys came over, offering to help however they could. One of the boys, Ross, is the same age as I am. It didn't take us long to become friends. Mrs. Barry brought a rhubarb pie which we shared once the tent was up and our "camping out" essentials were unloaded from the schooner. The six boys and I got a fire pit ready by scraping away the sod and hauling in some downed branches from the woods close by. One of the boys took the ax and cut the limbs into lengths ready for the pit. The rest of us stacked what he cut in a neat pile. We put the brush from these limbs in a heap over the pit to be burned first to clear the area. Another of the boys, Keith I think, fashioned two limbs that were in a *y* shape, along with a support for the kettle. The two *y* shapes were to be dug into the ground once the brush burned to hold the horizontal support for the kettle. This way, Mom could have a soup or stew brewing or a kettle of hot water ready. As we finished the kettle support, I saw something spooky out of the corner of my right eye.

In the area of the woods we had just picked over for downed wood, a man stood in this cleared area with an ax in his hand. I asked one of the Barry boys if he knew this man and was told it was Mr. Blaisdell. I was warned to stay away from him because he was crazy. Neil, the oldest Barry boy, had to go before he could tell me much about him. All too soon the Barry family left, promising to come back as soon as Dad had cut enough sod to build the sod house.

Many nights before we came on the trail, Dad and Grandpa talked about the sod house built when Grandpa John and Anne first homesteaded. From these discussions, Dad knew that to build our soddy, we needed the right kind of grass, a grass that had packed roots to hold the soil better. Dad knew that the prairie grass and blue grass that covered some of our land which would become field for crops had strong roots and would be best for the walls.

The first step in making the sod sections was to cut the sod lengths with a "grasshopper" plow that Dad borrowed the next morning from the Barry family. This plow cut four inch thick strips of sod into 12 inch widths. Dad used a spade to cut the strips into 12 inch "blocks". Some people used longer strips, making the building process go faster, but Dad knew that the square blocks made a neater building and were easier to handle when the doors and windows were framed in. Because Dad wanted to build Mom a three room house, he wasn't quite sure how many strips would be needed. It didn't matter if he cut too many because he knew he was clearing the land that would be our field anyway.

We cut and hauled the sod on the new two wheeled cart that Dad made for Benji, our paint horse. It seemed like the job would never end! If it weren't for the Barry boys, I think we would still be hauling those blocks from the field! When Dad said he thought we had cut enough sod, I jumped up and clicked my heels! I was tired of living in the tent and hauling sod. No one had any room for themselves in that tent ever!

That lack of room is part of the reason I built the fort over by the trees. I picked a spot where an old cottonwood had fallen. I also used most of that trunk for my back wall. I used the downed tree branches, logs and limbs I found in our woods. From the branches, logs and limbs I built walls the best I could around the trunk. Then, I proceeded to fill in all cracks and crevices with mud and small branches just like the beavers do. Last, I laid logs across the top. They seemed so heavy to move and lift at the time. It was all I could do to finish the roof in one day. The next morning after chores, I collected pine boughs and wove them into the roof. I knew it wouldn't hold all the rain out, but it made me feel like it was a little home of my own. I knew I could sleep here any time of year in any type of weather with any of my friends. The tent we lived in was as crowded as the schooner, so I often slept out in my fort during the time before the soddy was built. When the Barry boys came over, Ross and I sneaked over to my fort to shoot marbles or spin our tops to get away from our Moms and Dads and the older boys who ordered us around as "go fers" most of the time. We spotted Nise and Neil deep in conversation when we came out. I wonder if she is taking a "shine" to him!

Today I learned what "go fer" really meant! When I got up, Dad had staked out where the walls were going and had laid the first row of sod blocks down. He and Mom were walking arm-in-arm through the "door" he had planned. Six long, sturdy poles stuck in the air, four at each corner of the house with two in the middle that would support the entire roof. These poles would anchor the wood and sod roof, helping hold the walls in place.

As Mom went back to washing clothes with Nise and getting food ready for the Barry clan that she knew was coming to help that day, I started lugging the blocks of sod Dad had already cut, handing them to him so he could *build* the house. Sometime, maybe when I was sleeping at night, Dad made a door frame and door. He'd also spent some of our cash and bought four windows from McConkey's store. We brought some window panes with us in the schooner, but they were too hard to get at without unloading everything. The windows and door that Dad bought were propped up against a tree, ready to put in place as the walls "grew." Dad and Grandpa had cut trees into 1 x 4's too, and those were lying close by for framing. Murphy was the messenger for Mom and Dad. He kept coming around asking if Dad needed Mom to know anything. Most of the time, he came to tell Dad when Mom

20

had some food ready for us to eat.

We were very glad to see the Barry boys and their dad come to help with the construction. Mr. Barry has helped build many of the sod houses in Maine, so Dad was glad to have him. My job was to help carry sod. Two of the oldest Barry boys cut the blocks and the rest of us hauled to our dads who placed each block layer by layer, overlapping each sod block like a brick layer would. The door frame was propped in place and the blocks were butted against it as the wall grew. Windows were added in the same fashion.

Dad and Mr. Barry spent some time discussing how to make the inside walls, roof support and door frame between rooms work. While they were talking, we younger boys decided to go down by the Red River (Otter Tail) that runs across a corner of our homestead and close to the soddy. We wanted to check on the fish and hunt for some bullfrogs the other boys had heard "singing" during the night. Ross was sure that the frogs were fist size. I didn't believe him because he has huge hands. I was wrong! When we got there, we saw five monsters sitting on a log that stuck out into the stream of the river. Those big frogs reminded me of the Mark Twain story I once read about a frog jumping race. Each frog jumped in as we came close and swam away. There is always something new at the river. I could spend hours down there if I didn't have to work so much as we try and get settled in as a family in this new area. I heard Dad calling so we all scurried back to see what was happening at the building site.

When we all came back from the river, we saw Dad and Mr. Barry had set two ridge poles inside in the center of the house by digging a hole to put the pole in, much like putting a fence post in the ground. Dad had set the outside poles in the same way. These inside poles would help support the wood and sod roof and be a guide for building the inside walls too.

21

We cut, hauled and stacked the blocks all day. When Mom called us for each meal, I was amazed how much food she had ready and how much all the Barry boys and their dad ate. It must be a lot of work to feed a large family all of the time. Mom is busy most of the time and we are a small family. Mrs. Barry must never sleep! I bet she wishes some of those boys were girls so she had someone to help her like Mom has Nise. Once we had eaten, it was back to work hauling again.

Neil Barry asked me to tell Dad we were running out of the thick sod to cut and haul but Dad wasn't worried. The last row was in place and it was time to anchor the walls with the 1 x 4's. Dad and Mr. Barry laid the boards across the top of the last layer of sod blocks. Dad had brought along some long metal nails to use to toe in the boards to the poles. Wind storms were a worry for Dad and he did not want the roof to "fly off" during a storm. Once the "anchors" were in place, we quit for the night! It had been a long day for all of us, hauling and stacking. Dad knew Mom was tired as well, making all the food. The Barry clan climbed in their wagon and left, saying they would be back in the morning to help "raise the roof." That sounded pretty good to me. I wanted to see Ross again. We had fun down by the river.

Morning came too early for me. Dad had to yell at me twice this morning! I was so tired from all the lugging yesterday. Usually, I am a "willing worker" but I wasn't so willing today. I knew that we still had more sod lugging to do to get the roof on. When the Barry family came this time, their Mom was along, bringing some wonderful baked strudel and cookies. Mom was glad to have her help, and the two of them began to cook and plan the meals for us.

Walking over to the stacked boards that Grandpa John helped cut last year, Dad and Mr. Barry took the 1 x 4's and laid them on the ground, measuring the length needed to make the roof. The wood framing and rafters got really long and heavy, because Dad made the house a three-roomer. We built two sections of roof in this way and then the struggle began. It's a good thing that those Barry boys spend a lot of time wrestling each other. We needed their strength! Picking up each section and getting it up on top of the walls of the soddy was not an easy task. Once the two older boys, Mr. Barry and Dad got each section of the roof in place, the two older boys held it while Dad and Mr. Barry anchored each section to the poles. Dad was sure glad he had spent the money on those long nails. Wood nails would not have held this heavy roof very well at all. As soon as the two roof sections were anchored, it was time to lug some more sod blocks to build the wall up to the peak in the roof on each end. Just as we were done, Murphy came running to tell us it was "coffee time" so we all went over to the tent to see what the ladies had ready for us. Mrs. Barry's strudel was wonderful, full of June-berries, sweet and good. After eating, Ross and I tried to sneak off but were caught and told to hang around.

More "go fer"ing was needed. It was time to cover the roof with sod. Neil went back to cutting and we started lugging again. I wondered why Dad had us cut some of the sod thinner than the rest. Now I know! It was these thinner pieces that Neil cut and we carried to lie on top of the roof, once we put the tar paper Dad bought at McConkey's store over the rough sawn boards. Tar paper between the 1 x 4's and the thinner sod would cut down on the leaks. Adding the tar paper was expensive, but Dad wanted Mom to be comfortable until the log house got built. He wasn't sure how long we would have to live in the soddy. He needed to break the ground for fields and a get a shelter ready for the animals. Those tasks had to be done before the log house was built.

Chapter

4

Moving in

It is a fun time for me living in that soddy. I am sure it wasn't that much fun for Mom who has to keep it clean with the dirt floor and the "critters" large and small that are always about. Mice and spiders don't really bother me.

Snakes are another matter! I hate them, and a fair amount of them are always around with the Red River running across one corner of our homestead here. Because the walls are thick, the heat from the kitchen stove and Mom's cooking keep the house warm. It took a while for the fresh cut sod to dry out so the smell of wet earth and those little "critters" were around a little while too. Mom could have had a wood floor in our soddy, but she knew that Dad would build the log house as soon as he could. Sweeping the floor is Murphy's job. He has chores too, even though he is only five.

Our soddy is big compared to many in the area. Dad wanted to build a three roomer! To the left as you come in our front door are the two bedrooms. On the right is the kitchen with table, cupboard and stove. Dad is quite the carpenter. He used sawn off five-foot lengths from a large basswood log, wedged off four thick slices from it and planed them smooth on one side. Two of these he fitted snugly flat against each other, pegging them together with cross-wise slabs underneath to make a tabletop five feet long and about thirty inches wide. He bored two-inch holes six inches in from the corners, each slanted at a measured angle. Into these holes he drove oaken legs, shaped and sized to fit, sawed flush the extending board and sawed the legs off level, making a table! Not done, he made benches of the other slabs and two square-topped stools in the same way. The table and benches will crowd the soddy now but will be nice to have when the log house is built. Dad and Mr. Barry fashioned a shelf that runs around the kitchen walls about 12 inches down from the roof line. Now, we can unload all the things that Mom uses to cook from the schooner.

With the shelf in place, Mom and Mrs. Barry served supper to "the crew." The wild turkey Dad shot late last night and got ready on the spit for Mom to cook tasted wonderful. Mom used some of her rice and made gravy too. Mrs. Barry brought some canned vegetables she shared. We had lots of fresh milk to drink and butter to smear on the warm bread. Betsy, our cow, is a good producer! It is nice to enjoy extra treats like fresh butter. Many people have to use lard to spread on their bread. Somehow, Mom found time to bake bread over the coals of the spit. She usually makes desserts too. This time she had a bread pudding ready. I like it with cream on top. Yum!

Supper was a wonderful time of talking about the area and what we could expect. After supper, Keith and Wesley, two of the Barry boys, did the dishes. This duty was one of their assigned chores at home so their mom made sure they did their chore at our house too. When the dishes were done, the Barry clan boarded their wagon and headed home. As they left, Dad reminded Mr. Barry that we owed them help and intended to repay them whenever they asked. Clean up after the "roof raising" Dad decided had to wait until daylight.

Waking up to a bright, sunny day, Dad and I spent most of the next morning picking up and stacking the leftover sod and lumber. Mom and Nise were busy washing clothes. Seems like they are always washing something! We are lucky to be so close to the Red and a source of water. Mom is a stickler about keeping clean, doesn't matter if it's the house, our clothing or our bodies. We each have to take a Saturday night bath and sometimes a midweek one too, depending on the time of year. I usually go down to the Red and swim a while if the weather and water is warm enough to do so without me freezing.

Murphy went out to "hunt" - what he calls chasing frogs - in the long wet grass close by the house. He came back yelling at the top of his lungs. We thought something happened to him. Then he pointed down the road. We all were surprised to see Grandpa John come up the road to our house. He came to help us build the sod house and was amazed to see it already built *and* at its size. He grew up in a one-roomer soddy in Northwestern Norway. That one roomer was home for my Grandpa and Grandma and Grandpa's four sisters! After we all sat and talked a while as a family – Mom, Dad, Nise, Murphy and I – and shared some of Grandma's donuts, Grandpa helped us unload the schooner.

It's amazing how much we had packed on that schooner and how much room there is in our soddy. The bags and boxes of meal, potatoes, brown beans, dried peas, sugar, salt, black pepper, coffee, rice, onions, dry yeast and spices all found a place in Mom's small cupboard and kitchen area, once the cupboard was put in place in the kitchen. Molasses, vinegar, lard, fat salt pork and a small keg of herring in brine came in next for storage. Matches and tallow candles, the black iron cooking pot Mom uses on the stove, another stone crock, two large earthen bowls Mom uses when she bakes bread or makes larger quantities of something, the coffee mill, and our wooden dasher churn to make butter – each was placed handy for Mom to use. Grandpa showed Mom how to hang some of her pots that she didn't have shelf space for from the ceiling on ropes.

By the time we were all done unloading, Mom was glad that Dad and Mr. Barry had hung that shelf a couple nights ago. Mom found a place for most of what we brought with us. The two wooden wash tubs and copper boiler were left on the schooner. There just wasn't room for them in the little soddy kitchen area even with that shelf and cupboard. When the root cellar is dug and finished, some of the supplies like the onions and seed potatoes will be down there; but for now, all of the seeds and the staples we brought are in the soddy.

I asked Mom if I could sleep late in the morning since we had done so much today and she reminded me that there was more to do. Dad's tools used so far and those on the schooner yet (his carpentry tools and the scythe, rake, etc.

for farming) needed a permanent home. Next would be to build the lean-to barn that would have an area for the animals and another area for Dad's tools. Seems like there is *always* something to do.

Chapter

5

Building the Lean-to

        Once we had out of the schooner what Mom wanted, Dad moved the wagon closer to where the lean-to barn was to be. Since there were quite a few lengths of rough-cut 1 x 4's left, Dad and Grandpa laid out the framing for a home for the animals and Dad's tools. The long poles again were dug into the ground to form the footings for a rectangle. Grandpa John brought more nails, realizing we probably were running short by now. He and Dad began from the bottom up to attach the 1 x 4's to the poles, overlapping each board just a little. I was amazed that there was enough lumber to cover three sides of the barn and the roof too! It was dark before the three walls were done. Tomorrow means somehow dividing the space inside the lean-to so the animals have stalls of sorts and Dad's equipment still in the schooner will find a "home."

Tomorrow came too early again! Grandpa and Dad were up at the crack of dawn. Mom shook me about 6:30 AM and I protested but it didn't work. I was needed as "go fer!" I prayed Ross would just happen to come over so I wouldn't be the only one running for stuff. The two of us planned to fish the Red for some crappies we saw when we met at McConkey's store yesterday. I even dug worms so I'd be ready if he came. It was not to be.

When I got to the lean-to barn, I saw Grandpa and Dad were busy making four stalls for the animals on one side of the lean-to. I knew the other side would be for the equipment and grain storage. Once the stalls were done, shelves were made using the ends and pieces from the 1 x 4's along with a workbench. Two grain bins were sectioned off across the back also. Finally we could finish unloading the schooner.

Unload we did! Off came the grass scythe, snatch, square bottom spade, spare clevises, some draw-pins, the grub hoe and garden hoe, another adz, a broad axe, some steel wedges, plus a extra cow bell that rattled all the way here. Next we took out a one-man cross cut saw, crow bar, a steel file Grandpa gave Dad, the whetstone to sharpen dull blades, manila rope, strap hinges, a door latch, two window frames for the log house and four 8 X 8" panes for light in other areas of the house. Then came a few bolts, wood screws, a wood pail with a lid to carry water or feed, the tallow-tar mix for the wagon wheels, some square cut nails, and three empty nail kegs. Grandpa and Dad had made a false bottom in the schooner to hold most of what we unloaded. There was no McConkey's Store the first time Dad came and bought the contract for the land so he made sure we had the necessities with us. That all of this plus the kitchen stuff was on the schooner and that we all five slept in it when the weather was bad is truly amazing! The lean-to barn keeps the animals warm and Dad's tools protected from the weather just like our sod house does us.

The animals seem to like their places in the lean-to barn. For now, each has a place to bed down and be fed. Dad has a water trough just outside the lean-to to catch rainwater coming off the roof. He also put a barrel close to the house.

The day Grandpa left, Dad went to McConkey's store and bought some wire so we could fence an area close to the barn to keep our animals from wandering into town. The ewes especially were so used to the people we ran into coming up the trail to here that they just wander off now, often into Maine, and I have to go and herd them back. When Dad unloaded the wire he brought home in the back of the cutter, I knew I wouldn't be fishing today either. I am Dad's right hand man and need to be handy to help when he needs it. From the pile, it seemed like he had brought enough to fence the whole forty!

We took three of the long poles from the stacked pile and cut them into fence post lengths. The ground had hardened quite a bit from the sun and lack of rain, so digging nine holes for the posts was not easy. This soil is sandier so the water seeps away. The soil hardens quite easily from lack of moisture. We both spent most of the day digging, wrestling with the rocks that were where the posts were to go. Finally we could string the barb wire.

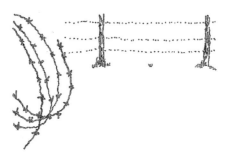

Once we were done with the fence, we let the horses and cows run untethered but kept the ewes tied. I told Dad I was done chasing them back home for a couple of days. I'm sure the men in line waiting to get grain ground at the mill heard the bleating. Mom came out and asked us if we were punishing the sheep. The noise lasted until we were out of sight and then they quieted down, eating the grass around them.

While Dad and I fenced the area for the animals, Mom made a salve for cuts, sores and blisters from too tight shoes, etc. Once not long ago a Medicine Man stopped to sell healing herbs. He taught Mom how to make the salve. I watched her make it one time later when I cut myself with my knife really deep. She takes a cup of lard and places it in a pan to melt. When melted, she adds a cup of ground ivy, not poison ivy but ivy that grows wild and twines. This is left to cook slowly for about 30 minutes – or until the ivy is "fried to a crisp". Mom takes a piece of cheesecloth and strains the liquid into a jar with a tight fitting lid, storing it in the root cellar when we don't need it so it keeps cool. I guess she thought she had better be ready in case someone gets hurt.

The salve works on the animals as well. One of the Belgians unused to the wire fence managed to get cut. Lena must have had an itch and she scratched herself open on the barbs. That ivy salve worked its wonders on her, and she was healed up in a very short time. Open sores are no fun and get infected so easy. I seem to get scratched daily from something. I hope that Medicine Man is right and that salve works as well on me next time I get scratched.

Chapter

6

Sod House Living

Most soddies in the area have fireplaces for heat and cooking. The stove we brought with us serves as our stove to cook on and heat for our home when it is cold until we build the log house. We weren't going to use the stove until we moved into the log house, but Mom decided it was necessary once she realized that the chimney would not be a fire hazard in the soddy.   I like the smell of the wood burning in the stove.   The smoke goes outside through the chimney pipes Dad and Mr. Barry fed through the roof. When I complained about having to haul wood into the wood box each morning and night one time Grandpa was here, I was glad that I wasn't raised on the western Dakota prairie.   Grandpa told me that one of his sisters gathers "buffalo chips" or dried manure plops for fuel. She lives in northwestern Dakota where there are few trees for fuel so buffalo chips become their fire fuel.   I can't imagine doing that and not coming home stinking of manure. I would think the burning manure would smell too. I guess it doesn't according to Grandpa.

I'd rather smell the wood or other food smells from Mom's cooking. Along with a tea kettle for warm water, Mom often has a kettle on the back burner with soup or stew brewing, never knowing who comes to the door wanting a meal

The heat from the stove also heats our bedrooms. I have the top bunk in the bedroom I share with Murphy and Nise, my older sister who is 15, until we get the log house built. Mom has hung a sheet across the room between the bunks and Nise's bed to divide the room, giving us some privacy that way. Murphy sleeps on the bottom bunk so if he tumbles out on the dirt floor, the fall isn't far. He sleep walks when he is overtired and needs to be close to the floor. Nise has a cot on the other side of the room and sheet divider. We all slept on hay on the floor for a few days until Dad was able to get the beds built, saving the new mattresses until we could put them on the cots.

Room is sparse but we all know that it is temporary so we try not to fight too much for space. Sometimes I still go and sleep in my fort, especially if it is warm out. James Flying Eagle, my Chippewa hunting partner, "Wing" (the name he goes by), scared me one day when I was out on our back forty. I was checking my traps to see if I had caught a fox in the new trap Dad had just bought me at McConkey's store. While I was bending over looking at the set trap to see if it had been disturbed at all, I felt a tap on my shoulder. When I looked over my shoulder, I got so scared at first that I almost stuck my hand in the trap! Wing talked to me in English which was another surprise, telling me not to be afraid. I learned later that he goes to Indian school and is taught the American language there. He was out looking for his pet dog, Hunter. Hunter had spooked a deer while they were walking and chased it towards our homestead. I told him that any time he was in the area and wanted to use my fort to rest or sleep, he was welcome. He showed me a trick to setting fox traps. They need to be covered a certain way so that "old wily" doesn't suspect it being there. We often run into each other now when we both are out hunting, especially on the back part of the homestead. The two of us haven't stayed overnight together in the fort yet, but plan on doing so soon. Sometimes, Ross and Mellie, my fishing buddies are able to come over and sleep out with me. We end up having a "hoot!" I have to be careful about what I say about Wing. Both Ross and Mellie don't like Indians and can't understand why I spend time with him.

The bunks in our sod house bedroom are more comfortable than sleeping on pine needles at the fort because they are made from some sturdy, straight poplar trees, cut and notched so that the ropes which are strung crisscross fashion hold the straw mattresses. The single bed that Nise sleeps in is made the same way. We brought the mattresses from Grandpa's when we moved up here. Grandma made them for us from the corn stalks that Grandpa grew last year. The mattresses are covered with a ticking material so they are pretty comfortable, especially since they are brand new. Mom and she made the quilts on all our beds.

Our bedroom has little in it except for some hooks to hang our clothes on and a shelf for each of us for our belongings. My shelf has my knife, slingshot, and my first trapped fox fur pelt. Murphy's shelf has his wooden toy wagon Dad made for him and a top that Grandpa made for him. Nise's shelf is cluttered with "girl" things like her hair ribbons, the sewing kit Grandma Anne gave her, and an old doll she brought with her from our former home. She has a simple flute that she plays when we have families visiting or we have a church "sing-along."

Most important, we have a "thunder pot" that we use during the night when it is cold and stormy out so we don't have to go out to our outhouse. None of us need much shelf space. We don't have many extra clothes and most of our time is spent helping around the homestead as much as we can. There is little time to play with toys of any kind.

Mom and Dad's bedroom is much the same as ours except that Mom brought with her on the wagon a chest that she was given by Dad that he made for her as a wedding present when they married. It has four drawers for her and Dad's clothing and treasures. Their bed is made a little longer than most since Dad is so tall, but it is made the same way as ours only wider to be comfortable for them.

To keep our soddy cleaner, Mom covered the walls with muslin so that the dirt from the sod sections and the "critters" aren't able to get in as easily. She did the same with the ceiling. Since the roof is grass thatched and sod over the 1 x 4's Dad used, it was more work to build but less likely to leak in a heavy rainstorm. Both coverings help to keep the place clean. Our floor is dirt but is very hard like a wood floor would be, hardened from walking on it so much. Murphy can't understand why he has to sweep twice a day. Dirt is dirt to him. He keeps asking Mom why he has to sweep inside when the outside dirt is never swept. Sometimes Mom puts rushes on the floor, giving us a carpet to walk on.

Most neighboring sod houses, except for the store and cheese house in Maine, are one room, quicker to build. It took us four days to build our house, even with all the help the Barry's gave us. The hardest part was to fill all the chinks in the walls where the sod blocks didn't quite mesh. Dad fixed some kind of a mud mixture that Mr. Thomas uses at the mill to fill holes in the mill structure. Sometimes we had to use rags and this mixture because the "holes" around the doors and windows were larger and needed extra caulking. This caulking process took Mom, Nise, Murphy and me one whole day! We were really glad when we were finished, able to take a bath and get all the "mud" off ourselves.

Our sod house is different from most. Most homesteaders find a hillside and build the soddy and cellar into it, eliminating the difficulty of any dividing walls like we have and getting them to stand straight using the support poles. Building in the hillside means less sod has to be cut and there is protection from the weather. Our home is protected from some of the wind and weather by the trees behind it, which will be important to have when the cold winter winds blow. Mom and Dad will "hire out" our soddy once we have the log house built. That's another reason we built a three-roomer. New people in the area are always looking for a place to stay until they find acreage to homestead. Mom may even agree to "hire out" overnight rooms for the people who come to the mill and need a place to stay while waiting in line for their grain to be ground.

Right now, our whole house smells onions! Mom found out that Mrs. Thomas is suffering from bronchitis, according to Dr. Pittitt, our local doctor here in Maine. Mom took some of her sweet onions we brought with us, cut them up fine, added a little bacon for taste and put them into a pot filled with water. The soup has been simmering a while, I know, or the smell wouldn't be so strong. Our family has used this remedy for *ever*, I think. My great grandma, Marie, treated Dad this way when he got bronchitis as a kid. Mom asked me to hang around so I could deliver the soup. I was glad to do it. This way, I get a chance to go to McConkey's and see what's been going on in town. I never know what I am going to hear. The world is sure changing fast.

Chapter

7

Meeting the stage

Mom got a real surprise today. When the stage came in to Maine, the driver unloaded a crate that had six chickens and a rooster in it. Was she happy! I just happened to be there when the stage rolled in, since I just finished delivering the onion soup to Mrs. Thomas. I was able to carry the crate home by making arrangements to come back tomorrow to pay for them since McConkey paid the driver for me. All this time Mom has traded milk and cream for eggs at McConkey's store. Now, she will be able to sell the milk and cream or barter for other supplies she needs.

Whenever I get the chance, I go to the store or the mill. I like the store best. The smells of all of the spices, dried meats, candy treats like licorice, and coffee in bins make my mouth water. The chickens mean we now have to build a coop for them so the fox in the area don't get free dinners. Dad got busy and made a small coop that has a special rear door to reach in and pick eggs. If the door is lifted high enough, it is very easy to clean the floor. This hinged door made replacing the old straw on the floor with new much easier too. Dad saw the coop plan in the *Weekly* down at the Mill one day when he was helping repair a broken wood section of the grinder. Dad is always asked to help at the mill because of his experience in carpentry and knowledge of machinery too. Thomas knows that Dad works hard and will help however he can to get things running again. Whenever I see Thomas at the mill, he reminds me that if I work as hard as my father at whatever I do, I will be a successful person.

We drop the door down on our coop and latch it, making sure the hinged door in back is hooked shut each night. One of Murphy's jobs is to check the coop just before dark to make sure all six "cluckers" and the rooster are "put to bed." If he can't find one or two, I have to take my slingshot, locate them and help him chase them home to the coop. If I take small pebbles and shoot them near the back of their feet, the chickens run to the coop for protection. Most of the time, I end up feeding and watering the chickens for Mom. That has become one of my many chores.

Being new and coming to this area before crop raising season, we needed to somehow feed and bed all the animals. Neighbors like the Barrys have been so good to us. Mr. Barry even loaned Dad sufficient hay, straw and grain to feed and bed the chickens and other animals until the first crops come in this summer. Dad plans to return all loans in full from the best quality that he gets from the harvest.

Mom, Nise or I milk and feed the cow and heifer, pick eggs and feed the chickens twice a day. Dad cleans the pens once a day, removing the dung and replacing it with fresh straw that Barry supplied. Dad piles the manure high on the side of the barn lean-to so it can be loaded on the horse cart Grandpa John helped Dad make last time he was here. The cart was made to help haul the dung for spreading on the new broken field before spring harrowing.

Dad came home from Maine and told Mom the "Minnesota Blizzard", Maria Blaisdell, who lives in Pelican Rapids, a town to the north and a little west from here, was visiting her brother and his wife, the Blaisdells. He is the same person I saw in the woods the day we built the soddy. Once Dad told his story, I knew why the Barrys told us to watch out for Mr. Blaisdell.

Dad brought home a copy of the newest newspaper in the area, the *Farmer's Alliance* printed in Henning, a small town to the southeast of here. The editor, Frank Haskins, is a bit "odd" too. Dad was told that sometimes in his editorials, Haskins attacks the banks and businessmen. On one occasion Haskins was sent before a justice of the peace who put him in the state hospital for the insane in Fergus Falls for his comments. At this same time, Maria Blaisdell was committed there, spending time in the institution as well. The two of them sued Otter Tail County for false imprisonment. They won their case and were released. Maria has been "a terror" ever since. Because

41

of her almost six foot height, she makes everyone jump when she begins to fret.

The neighbors claim that Maria Jane Blaisdell has always been a character. Maria thought she was special and became a nuisance to the important political leaders around the state and in Washington at the U. S. Capitol. Somehow, she did some sort of nursing at Fort Snelling during the Civil War. She insisted that the government owed her a pension for the nursing time. Not only that, over the last twenty years, she has been needling the congressmen to present a bill to raise the amount of that pension she thinks she should be getting! She has been so nasty and determined that anyone who sees her coming and feels forced in to dealing with her runs the other direction if possible, considering her a holy terror! If she corners someone like a congressman, he sits patiently and listens to her story, gives her a small sum of money and starts her on the way home, back to Pelican, hoping to get rid of her. Pelican people are glad to give her cash to *also* get rid of her for a while so they don't hear her ranting. Newspapers around the country call her the "Minnesota Blizzard," because she blows in and out of towns regularly. It is her brother I saw with the ax in the woods when we first came here. When there is work to do around his homestead, Blaisdell takes his ax and goes out into the woods. Often he is gone for hours on end. Usually when this happens and his wife discovers him gone, she goes to find him and brings him home. Quite regularly, we see Mrs. Blaisdell with the cart, driving up the road, calling his name, "John! John! Where are you?" I told Mom Blaisdell could use a cow bell!

Chapter

8

Living near Maine

Dad bought our forty acre homestead from the government in southeast corner of Section 35, Lot 8 in Maine Township for $1.25 per acre, paying a total of $50 for the land. If he had bought it from another person, it would have been $5 to $10 an acre. We think the land was a foreclosure sale so the government sold the land at a very reasonable price. About 20 acres are tillable. Ten acres of it are swamp and stream and really good for hunting and trapping. We also have 10 acres of woods that has good logs and lumber for building log homes, lean-to buildings, etc.

When Dad and Grandpa John first came to homestead this land, Dad put money down for the property. That same day, they started marking the trees that were to be cut for the log house. They knew that many trees would be needed for the buildings and fence to come later on. Since it costs 2 cents per foot for piled logs, and 3 cents a foot for sawn logs and square timbers, we save a lot of money by cutting them ourselves on our own land. It is better for the wood to age too. The beams and boarding will not twist so much if the lumber has a chance to weather and dry a little before building. We won't have so much trouble filling the chinks once the place is built either.

Our soddy is pretty comfortable. We will live in it until the house is built in the late spring or early summer, depending on how crop and garden planting go which must come first. Dad plans to build the sod house on the opposite side of the river where most of our acreage lies.

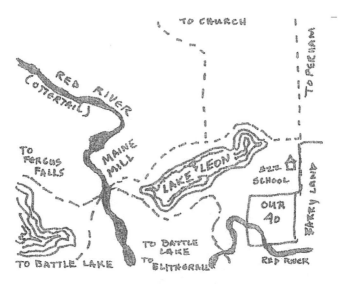

Dad decided to settle here because he heard when he came up to this area earlier looking for homestead land that Mr. Thomas was building the local flour mill along the Red River (Otter Tail) here in Maine. There are two small towns called Maine in the area, the other one just north of here. The poor stage driver gets so confused when he tries to deliver mail or any packages. The church we go to is located at the other Maine, about four miles north of here. There is a school there too, but the school we go to is just on the other side of the northeast corner of our forty on the road that goes to the other Maine. Our house is in the southeast corner of our forty. School is near the northwest corner, through field and woods.

The **Maine Roller Mills (Phelps Mill)**, about two miles west our sod house, has just begun operating here on the Red River (December 1889). Thomas had hoped to open earlier but weather and building problems delayed the start. Francis Mosher was its first customer. Mosher brought the very first sacks of grain to the mill on a bobsled driven by horse. The Roller Mill is one of eighteen mills in this area. This mill produces Gold Foil Patent, Silver Leaf Fancy and Baker's Choice flour.

I like to go down to the mill. The wheel that spins in the water weighs 7000 pounds! It is 70 inches wide and 18 feet around. I love to go and fish the millstream when neither Mom nor Dad has anything for me to do. Sometimes I get chased away from the mill, especially while it was just being built and Thomas and his helpers were moving in the heavy equipment. At other times, I am able to sit quietly and quietly listen to the men gossip and watch them work.   The mill runs most days from 7 AM to 10 PM, grinding grain into flour. When the mill gets busy, I help sew the sacks full of ground flour closed and Thomas pays me in copper pennies.

Thomas hates the muskrats that frequent the water around the mill. Because there is an area on the other side of the Red, across from the mill, that is slow moving, both muskrats and beaver are seen frequently.   Thomas pays 10 cents a rat for each one caught and shown to him. The minister's two sons often lie on the bank of the river opposite the mill, shoot a rat, bring it in to the mill and get paid by Thomas. Once they are paid, they take it back to the bank on the opposite side again, wait another hour and bring the same rat back. Mr. Thomas thinks it's a different rat and pays the boys again for the very same rat! I don't do that. Mr. and Mrs. Thomas are good people. Mrs. Thomas is one of my mom's new friends. I would not cheat either of them. Mr. Thomas recently moved a log house onto his property, and we all wonder what his plans are for it.

The stagecoach stops three times a week, sometimes in front of Thomas' mill. If there is a delivery of supplies for McConkey's store or there is mail for one of the homesteaders, it will stop at the store. Mr. McConkey is postmaster. There is talk of hiring someone to deliver the mail to each homestead in the area but it is just talk so far. I wonder if mail will be delivered like the Pony Express does out West. Probably the next thing we know the railroad will deliver mail. We already have a track close to here. Some of the land around here is owned by the railroad too. The railroad has finally branched through the entire state of Minnesota and some of the land around here is theirs. Many people travel by train if they can rather than by horse or stage. It is more comfortable, I guess, and somewhat quicker in times of hours on the road. I'm not sure it is any safer than the stage though. The papers have had stories of train robberies just like the stage. It must be risky to stop the train to rob it!

Logs are shipped by rail now instead of the old fashioned way of floating logs down the river. I hear the men at the mill talk and some of them claim that half of the logs and those nasty deadheads are still left in the rivers from when people floated them to the lumber mills the old fashioned way. They are hazards and create snags in the river flow.

Thomas earlier built the Farmer's Roost, a small cabin that has cots for the men who arrive late in the day and end up in a line, waiting to be the next mill customer to have grain processed. Next door to the Roost he also built a barn for the animals (oxen, mules, or horses) that bring the wagonloads of grain sacked.

Mom often sends me to the Roost with food to sell to the men. Her "spending money" for extras comes from the sales made to the men waiting to grind their grain. If they did not bring food with them, the only other place to get food is at McConkey's store. There is no hotel or place to eat so far here in Maine. If the cots are full at the Roost, Thomas has hay strewn in the corners where men can lie down to sleep. When the Roost is full, men come to the surrounding homes, asking if there is a place to bed for the night. If the wait is a day or more and the line is long, Maine residents negotiate a fee and let the farmers stay with them. "Hiring Out" rooms is what Mom and Dad hope to do with the soddy once we move into the log house. Very few neighbors have extra room so I am sure the soddy will be full most of the time.

Dad built an outhouse the same way he built the sod house. Ours is one of the few built of sod. Dad had enough sod left for the outhouse which will be used by those who hire out our sod house rooms if Mom decides to hire out rooms. He will build us another outhouse of wood closer to the log house when it is done.

A blacksmith shop is being built by Carl A. (Albert) Gabriel. It is a soddy too, located down the lane from his house. Gabriel hopes that farmers who bring in flour will bring their plowshares to sharpen or fix and have him shoe their horses and mules if that is needed. Gabriel knows that the mill will use him when the machinery breaks. A good blacksmith becomes everybody's friend. Many people are beginning to use metal nails instead of wood ones too. When business is slow, Gabriel makes nails for sale.

This rough land is hard on plowshares and any metal attachments due to those "winter potatoes" (rocks) that seem to grow out of the dirt. I remember Grandpa John, Dad, Nise, Murphy and I fighting with a rock by the windbreak on the edge of the field for what seemed like most of a week before we could finally hook up Lefty and Lena, our Belgians, to pull it out.

The community is thriving because of the mill activity. Mr. McConkey's store that he opened in 1887 is housed in a larger soddy with a wood addition. He has been ill and is trying to sell out but is not having too much success. It is amazing what is in that store! A glass case has Prince Albert, Copenhagen snuff and other tobaccos. Then there are glass containers of jelly, sago and tapioca in bulk, syrup and black molasses in covered pails, a bulk candy case and bulk cookie rack. That candy case is my favorite place of all to spend the copper pennies I earn sewing sacks closed. The crackers are in a cardboard box. Sugar and salt have special bins. McConkey even gets crates of apples and grapes in season.

Every three or four days, McConkey buys blocks of ice cut from Lake Leon behind the store each winter that are stored in sawdust in one of the cabins he owns close to the store. It is important for him to have ice for the icebox that stores salami, ring bologna, bacon, butter, lard, cheese, and ice cream makings. Peanut butter and cheese are scooped out of larger containers and put in the

48

customer's jars or tins which they bring to fill. The filled container is weighed on the scale and sold by the pound weight. McConkey has brooms on hooks, some hardware and drug items, sewing notions, horse collars, and limited clothing such as underwear. Most people go to Fergus Falls when they need shoes and fancy clothes.

A cheese house is due to open in April up the road and south of the Mill. Mom can't wait to have the luxury of buying bulk cheese instead of continuously making cheese herself for all the lunches or meals that she peddles to the mill's customers. It is probably cheaper for her to make our own cheese, however. It does take some time to cure cheese, so she often gets behind, finds herself without any for the lunches, and needs to buy some for sandwiches, etc.

School is two miles from here if I go the road. Dad sometimes lets me take the horse and the little cutter school when it is as cold as it has been recently. Nise and I just fit in the small seat. We have a lap robe made of horsehair and a foot warmer to keep us warm. Sandy Van Vlect is our teacher at Disctrict 22.

School has been closed for a few days. Last time school met, Denise and I were two of the three present. So many families have the grippe. We are 45 total students when we are all there at school. According to Dr. Pittitt, the best way to stop the spreading of the grippe is to stop gathering in groups, so Miss Van V. told us to stay home until she feels safer in having us gather. I was so glad. No school means Ross and I will have more time to fish or trap. Maybe Wing will be in the area and I will run in to him when I check the trap lines. He always has such interesting hunting stories to tell. Even though he is as young as he is, he is allowed to go out on the hunts when his Chippewa tribe is looking for game. I hope the tribe doesn't have the grippe or he will not be able to travel either.

I'm glad Grandma Anne sent the elderberry sauce and juice with us when we moved here. Dad fussed a little, trying to find room to store the jars in the schooner. Elderberries are a good cure for coughs, colds and sore throats. With the grippe around, it's nice to know we have some remedies that have worked before in case we get sick. I know when Grandma makes the *cure*, the juice is more berries than water, so it will be strong medicine.

Chapter

9

Soon Christmas

Since I still have no school because so many people have the grippe, I went out wandering today and scared up a handsome jack rabbit. I shot him with my slingshot and brought him home to Mom for supper. She asked me to spit roast him in the old pit area outside that we used when we first came on the schooner before we had the soddy built. She was busy baking bread and didn't have room in the oven.

Rabbits are easy to roast on a spit. I asked Mom for a small onion which she gave me. I had skinned and cleaned the rabbit already down by the river and rinsed it in the cold, icy water that was still flowing there before I brought it home. I got another pail of water, re-rinsed the rabbit again, making sure the inside was clean. Into the cavity I put the cut up onion, some button mushrooms Mom and I dried earlier, which I had found on the road back from the Red one time this fall, and some thyme that grows wild along the house that we also had dried. Spit roasting sounds complicated but isn't. The extra seasonings help to cover the "wild" taste. I put potatoes in the coals to bake too.

The spit is sheltered by a grove. It is a warm day with the sun out bright, not a bad day for December. Mom is also busy washing clothes and hanging the wet wash outside on a line Dad has strung. Once the clothes have frozen, Mom will bring them in and hang them around the soddy to dry. Freezing takes some of the wetness out of the clothes, making drying go faster.

Before school closed because of the grippe, we practiced for the Christmas program. I have a part in the Christmas play. I am one of the wise men. Ross is one of the kings and keeps asking me to "bow down!" Last time he did that, I gave him a friendly sock in the gut. I get to wear this tall, pointed hat and deliver a gift to the baby in the manger. We will also sell goodies after the play to buy more library books. I get to pop popcorn in the fireplace. I hope I don't burn it. Burned popcorn really stinks up a place!

Mom thinks we will have room for a very small Christmas tree in our sod house this Christmas. She is not sure we can put the candles on it. Because we are so crowded now in the soddy, we might bump a candle and light the tree on fire. I told her I didn't care so much about candles as I did about putting "sweet Angie the Christmas tree angel" up on top of the tree. I reminded her to make kringle too. It's a light pie crust kind of pastry crust that has an almond flavored frosting with slivered almonds sprinkled on top. Yum! Christmas wouldn't be Christmas if we didn't have kringle. Mom put new straw down on the floor once the old straw was taken out to the barn for bedding the animals. It will seem strange not to have any of our grandparents around for Christmas. This will be the first year in a long time that we will just be the five of us. I miss

Grandpa John the most. He is always full of wonderful stories.

I've been "on the hunt" for a big turkey for Christmas Eve supper. I shot and missed one yesterday. For as big as they are, they are fast and can fly enough through the trees to make aiming at them hard. Dad said I need to shoot in front of the bird, hoping that the turkey keeps going in the same direction as I shoot. I have a few more days yet to get lucky!

Darn! I was hoping Mom had forgotten. No such luck! Some of Mom's cures don't taste too bad; others are putrid! With the grippe making so many sick, Mom hunted in her medicine until she found the cod liver oil. Yuck! I know it is good for us but it tastes awful. Mom makes each of us take a teaspoon a day. I make sure I have some water ready to drink to wash the awful fish taste down afterwards. Even with the water, I gag. I hope it works. Sometimes I'd rather risk getting sick than taking it!

FIRE is a scary word anytime on the prairie. Last night I was helping Dad with the chores and saw smoke. I yelled at Dad to come and take a look. At first we thought it was an explosion of the grain dust at the mill. From the direction of the smoke we decided that it was coming from the Barry property next to us. I took a pail, ran to the house to tell Mom and took off down the path to the Barry's place. John's house had caught fire in the roof of the one wing where there's a chimney. The flames were only on the roof so we took buckets, set up two lines and two ladders to throw water onto the flames. We were lucky and were able to save the house structure. Only part of the roof burned off. Water leaked inside from the buckets of water thrown on the roof, but damage to the rest of the structure was not too bad. John was very happy that we came to help. I helped run the buckets back to the well once they were empty. We were fourteen of us. The well isn't far from the house so we didn't have to stretch the line too far. Nise and Mom came too and helped pass the pails of water down the line. Two of us ran empty buckets back. Mom and Nise stayed to help Mrs. Barry mop up the water inside the house once the Barrys felt the fire was out.

When the fire threat was over, Dad helped John cover the roof with canvas. Our old tent we used when we first came, the one we lived in for a while, got another use. Dad went home and brought the canvas over to help cover some of the house where the roof once was. Dad offered the squared logs that he has ready for our barn roof to Barry to use to rebuild his roof. Barry is coming over tomorrow, will get the squared logs, and will either pay Dad or replace them. He was grateful that we could offer the use of the logs to help his family out. This way he can get the roof back on quickly and the family will not be so cold – after all, it is January – and they won't have to stay with someone until the logs are cut and the roof gets rebuilt, nor will they have to worry about snow accumulating on the canvas roof and caving into the house. Dad volunteered that he and I would come and help when we finish chores in the morning after the logs are loaded and moved.

Because so much of the bedding and blankets got wet, Mom asked the Barrys to come and sleep at our house for the night. When we first moved here, they were so kind to us, offering sleeping space and food until we got settled in our tent those first few days on our new homestead. They accepted Mom's offer, not knowing how cold it would be with the roof just canvas. That means that Murphy, Nise and I will sleep on blankets on the floor. We haven't done that since the first night the sod house was built and we hadn't moved in our things from the schooner.

Chapter

10

Mr. Barry Brings News

Mr. Barry brought over a copy of the *Fergus Falls Weekly*. He saw our name in the paper dated January 2, 1890. Our name was on a list of letters that were unclaimed in the post office in Fergus Falls, Otter Tail County, Minn., as of December 24, 1889. To get the letter we have to go to Fergus Falls and pay 1 cent for the letter. If we don't go and get the letter within 14 days, it will be sent to the dead letter office wherever that is, never to be retrieved. Dad plans to take Mom and me by sleigh one day before the time is up. I have grown out of my shoes and have blisters from the old ones. Mom wants to make me some new pants and shirts. There is a better fabric selection in the two stores that sell piece goods in Fergus than is available at McConkey's store. Space is limited in McConkey's store so he has to be careful what he stocks. I have grown so much in the last six months. Everything I have to wear is too small. I've had to wear some of Dad's clothes until she can make me new.

That same paper had an advertisement for a "potato culture apparatus used to mash the lumpy soil in the bottom of the trenches" for the potatoes. The "potato culture" or trencher is drawn by either two horses or a single horse and is used to "mellow up" the soil. I hope we get one to make breaking the ground Dad wants to use the culture to make planting potatoes this spring easier. The horse is hooked to the front part to the right of the handles.

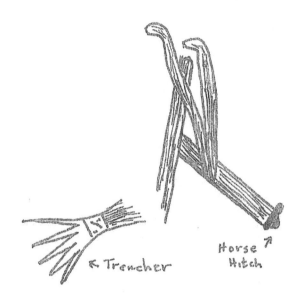

← Trencher   Horse ↗ Hitch

The tine portion connects to the up and down board, which tips backward and "rakes" across the ground, smoothing out all the rough areas as the horse pulls forward. Dad wants to see if he can order one. He and Mr. Gabriel (Albert) at the blacksmith shop want to start making them to sell in the area. The soil here when it is first broken or turned over is hard to cultivate. A lot of rocks turn up as we take the top sod off and we clear the trees and shrubs so we can plant the grains. Dad is a good carpenter and with Albert's help, they could have a thriving business selling the culture to other homesteaders breaking new land for crops.

Dad brought home the *Weekly* he found left at the Roost. Usually I am the one who finds a copy. In it were instructions on how to make a good harrow. He is excited to show the harrow picture to Albert too and see if the two of them can produce both the potato culture and harrow to sell in the spring for land tillage. I hope they have success making the harrow as well as the potato culture. Albert and Dad could ship the machinery to neighboring towns by stagecoach and train. If the harrow and potato culture sell well, Mom can stop filling lunch pails for spending money. Dad will be able to give her spending money from the sales. He'll probably have to hire out the fields to a neighbor for a percentage of the crop so he can spend his time carpentering. The harrow is a little more work and a little larger to ship, but Albert and Dad think it will catch on, making land tilling easier.

Dad does the splitting, sawing, hewing, planning, bolting and carving of the oak for the harrow and culture.

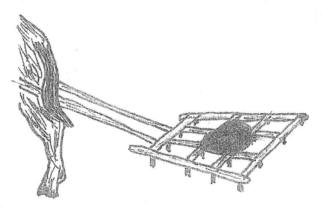

Albert forms the teeth for the culture and welds them to another piece of metal that screws into the upper wood structure. Sometimes Dad uses wood pegs; other times he

57

uses nails that Albert forms. Albert makes all the nails and metal parts. The stronger metal nails cause less breaking of equipment. Less time is spent repairing and more work can get done.

The harrow needs thirty pegs or nails. Dad and Albert will send spare nails along if someone buys one in case a nail breaks or works loose. The harrow is also used to loosen and smooth the soil once it has been broken with a plow. The stones, hidden just under the ground, cause the pegs or nails to break or loosen. Most farmers go first one way (north and south) and then the other (east and west) or vice versa to work the ground for planting.

Chapter

11

Indian Visitors

Dad and I went to Albert's place today so Dad could show Albert the plans he has drawn for the harrow. I like to go to the blacksmith shop. Albert always has the fire blazing hot, ready to make or mend whatever is ordered or comes in the door to be fixed. Dad and Albert were very intent on discussing the plans so I asked if I could head on home. Knowing how I like to be down at the mill, Dad told me I had to be home by supper to feed the animals. I agreed.

When I walked outside, I noticed some smoke coming out of the woods in the direction of the Barry place. I decided to go over for a look-see. The smoke wasn't coming from the Barry place at all. I stumbled upon two Chippewa Indians camping on Barry's land. I was a little scared when I saw the two Indians, but I soon found out I had no reason to be frightened. The brave's name was Walks-With-Wolves and his son who was with him was called Little Wolf. Little Wolf spoke good English because he was attending a mission school on the reservation. He knew Wing, my friend. I now know why Wing hasn't been around lately to see me from what Little Wolf told me about the reservation conditions. When we talked, I found out Little Wolf was about two years older than I am. He also told me why they were camped on Barry's land.

They left the reservation to hunt and search for food, because the government beef that was supposed to be sent to the reservation has not arrived. Many of the people in the tribe are hungry. The Indians had a very lean summer, but the tribe managed to live through the summer and fall on a lot of fish that they netted from the lake on the reservation. The wild rice that grew in an area of the lake which they harvested using their canoes this late fall helped some but food is very scarce. The strongest braves are sent off the reservation in search of game and told to bring back as much as they can carry.

The two had put together a makeshift shelter, much like my fort. It was a cold January day, but it was warm around their campfire. Little Wolf is about the same height as I am but a little heavier. He is handsome and any girl would swoon over his copper skin and dark hair, I am sure. His father, Walks-With-Wolves, is fierce looking, dressed in skins, and has hand-made moccasins on his feet. He wears a single feather in his hair. That is all that *covers* his head, even in this cold weather! I could tell by their body actions that each had a strong love for the other.

I was so excited to have a newcomer in the area and I asked if the two of us could spend some time together, maybe at my fort or hunting or fishing. Little Wolf asked me to keep their camping here in the woods a secret for a while. They were afraid of the mistrust between the settlers and Indians that was still around from previous battles mostly south of us. I said I would keep the secret but I knew it would be hard not to be able to tell Mom and Dad my news. I asked if I could come back on Saturday. I wanted to fish with him for some large crappies I knew were in Lake Leon. I told Little Wolf that I would have to do my chores first, including delivering Mom's meals to the mill. He asked his dad, smiled at me and agreed to meet again.

I woke up to a sunny and crisp Saturday morning, very cold like much of this January has been so far. I took the lunches after I finished chores and headed to the mill and Lake Leon. Little Wolf was already at the lake when I got there. Most times when I have been down at the lake, local people are usually fishing. Today there was nobody around. Little Wolf was happy to be there just with me, I could tell. It seemed to both of us that we had been friends for a long time. We fished for a while, catching quite a string! His eyes gleamed with our prize. He knew he would have some food to bring back to his tribe and was anxious to show his dad so we headed back across Lake Leon. I knew there were springs in the lake and told him to watch out for weak ice. I told him too that the men had been cutting ice blocks for storage to be used to keep food cold, that he should step lightly and watch for tree branches stuck in the ice - a warning sign that blocks have been cut.

I was about ten yards ahead of Little Wolf and almost on shore when I suddenly heard a loud cracking noise. I turned around and to my horror saw my new friend, Little Wolf, in the icy open water where the ice had opened up behind me! I didn't dare go back and try to get him out. I hollered at the top of my lungs for help! Almost right away, who should appear but Mr. Blaisdell with his ax in hand! Blaisdell quickly sized up the situation and cut a sapling. He extended this out to Little Wolf, who was able to grab it and pull himself out. I tried to get Little Wolf to go to the mill where I knew we would get help. He did not want to go there; so with Blaisdell half carrying him, we made our way back to their camp. Walks-With-Wolves set

61

about drying and warming Little Wolf. Since he did not speak English, Little Wolf had to translate for us when his dad spoke. His father told Blaisdell that he had saved his son's life. Because of this, Blasdell would forever be a brother to Walks-With-Wolves. Blaisdell was only too glad to have helped. As he left, Blaisdell asked me to keep this a secret between us because he did not want to ruin his "reputation." So much excitement for one day! I did not want to but knew I had to go home, wishing that I could tell Mom and Dad what had just happened. I knew that a "promise is a promise" so I kept it all "locked in my heart." I told Little Wolf that I would try and get back after church, tomorrow, to see how he was doing.

After church services, I did not get a chance to see my new friends because we were playing family games, something we usually did after church on Sundays. I couldn't figure out a good excuse to get out of the house, so I had no choice but to join in and have some family fun. Monday was school. Because it was so cold, Mom and Dad kept a close eye on Nise, Murphy and me for most of the week whenever we were out and about.

Finally, it began to warm at the end of the week. I hadn't even been to the mill all this time so I asked Mom and Dad if I could go "to town" and see what was going on. Mom said yes if I would get her some nutmeg and salt. I agreed fast and took off out the door before she changed her mind.

I went to the campsite first, hoping to see Little Wolf and check on how he was doing after the cold bath. I was so disappointed! I found their campsite deserted! I felt a real sense of loss and wondered what had happened to them. I tried to see Mr. Blaisdell but he was nowhere around either. I went to the mill, sat and listened for a while, went to McConkey's store and got the supplies for Mom, and headed on home.

While Mom was fixing supper and we were waiting for Dad to come in from chores, she said that a visitor came by while I was gone. It was the sheriff. He wanted us to know that there had been some Indians camped on Barry's homestead. The sheriff had "run them off" since they were camped on land that wasn't theirs. This made me feel so bad! I know all of this land belonged to the Indians at one time. Little Wolf told me that the reservation land that they now live on isn't the best. I felt bad also because Mom said that she was glad that "those people" were gone. I wish she could have met Little Wolf and his dad. I turned away so that the family would not see the tears in my eyes. I know that Little Wolf would have been a good friend. It made me very unhappy to know that I would probably never see him again. I learned a good lesson from this today - people are people, regardless of whatever differences we have. Each of us deserves the respect of the other, no matter what our skin color or family background is.

Chapter

12

Collecting Our Letter

Mom, Dad, and I all got in the wagon early yesterday morning and went to Fergus Falls to get that letter that was in the post office. Dad decided the night before that if the weather looked good in the morning, we would go. When we were done with chores, Dad thought the temperature was around 30 degrees above zero with little wind and a clear sky so off we went.

Fergus Falls is a bigger town and it was exciting for us to be there. It is built along the Otter Tail River and has many stores. I find myself walking the streets with my mouth open, looking in the store windows at the items for sale. There are even board sidewalks where the stores and rooming houses line the street. We bought shoes for me and fabric so Mom can make new pants and shirts. The kids at school are teasing me about my "high water" pants since I have grown so much.

Another of the stops was at F. J. Kneeland's City Drug Store. We had seen an advertisement in one of the *Weekly* papers for a horse doctor book he was giving away. Our Belgians have a skin rash from their collars. We will need them soon to pull the sledge when we bring the logs out of the woods for the log house. Mom thought that the doctor book might have a remedy to help heal their rash.

I was hungry and asked if we could stop and eat something somewhere. That was exciting! We went to one of the hotels and sat down in their eating area. The "special" of the day was a beef stew and homemade bread. Yum, was it good! Nise wasn't hungry so I ate hers too! That was one time I was glad to have a sister!

We finally went to the Post Office to get the letter once we had some dinner. By the postmarks on the outside of the letter, it has traveled farther than we have over the last eight months. It sure has taken a round about route to get to us.

The letter was from my Uncle Knute, Dad's brother who does not write often. His letters keep us up to date about his family. The first postmark was Medora, North Dakota. There were other town postmarks too but since this was dated first, we knew Medora was the place he mailed the letter. The North Dakota postmark was a change since the last letter. That previous letter was postmarked Dakota Territory. Dad told us that the Dakota Territory had just in the last year's time split into two states, North Dakota and South Dakota. Uncle Knute's letter was in my Aunt Hilda's handwriting. Uncle Knute does not know how to read and write. The letter read:

My Dearest Brother,
Greetings and love to you and your family. We wish God's blessing on you in your new home and wish all of you happiness and good health.

As for us, we have had a very hard year on the Dakota prairie. It was a severe winter for us, and we lost about half of our cattle in the big February blizzard. Robert (this is my oldest cousin) came down with the grippe and was very sick this early spring. Thanks be to God that as the weather warmed up he began to feel better. He is now back helping me with the cattle. We still get most of our supplies in the town of Medora.

The whole town and surrounding area are awed by the huge house - they call it a chateau - built by the Frenchman, Mqrquis de Mores. Medora is named after his American wife whose given name was Medora. The chateau is a grand place with fancy furniture and china or so we have been told by some of our neighbors who have been lucky enough to be invited there for supper. This is the same person who built a slaughterhouse so that area cattle could be butchered locally instead of shipped to the Eastern packing plants. His venture was not successful.

There are getting to be some good sized ranches in the area. The Maltese Cross Ranch south of Medora and the Elkhorn Ranch north of town are both owned by a conservationist and hunter, Mr. Theodore Roosevelt. He originally came here to hunt buffalo and became interested in cattle ranching. He is becoming very famous in these parts. "Teddy", as he is known, helped form the Little Missouri Stockman's Association and has been its most recent President and Chairmen of our association. Roosevelt is also a writer, having authored several articles. Rumors are he is working on a book about game found in western Dakota. The book is supposed to be about the habits and hunting of white tail and mule deer, mountain sheep, elk, buffalo, antelope, wolves, coyote, and grizzly bear, along with stories about grouse, ducks and geese. It is also rumored that he is becoming involved in politics, so it will be interesting to see if he ever runs for *a political office.   He is very popular with the cowboys on his ranches and is a very interesting individual to talk to.*

Life on the prairie continues to be hard.   With the loss of a lot of our cattle, we have had to borrow money at the bank to replace some of the stock.   We have been lucky to have had no prairie fires and hope for enough rain this summer so that the grasslands support our animals. Robert's horse, though, stepped in a prairie dog hole this spring and broke its leg. We had to put it down. Those pesky prairie dogs develop their own little "towns" and become a real hazard for our animals.

We hope to hear from you about your travels and your new home and wish you success on your homestead.

With love from you brother,
Knute (and Hilda)

We can tell from Uncle Knute's letter how hard things must be for him and his family.   We consider ourselves very lucky to have our land, animals and the things necessary to work our homestead debt free. Dad is a skilled carpenter and had enough money saved when we came for us to buy most of what we need until the new crops are harvested. Most of what the Barrys lent us when we came has been paid back too. The letter reminds us of our good fortune in having some money to get a good start when so many homesteaders struggle greatly just to "get by." Most homesteaders came West I have learned on a "shoe string" and do not have an outside skill like carpentry to fall back on to help pay bills when the crops are not good or the animals get sick and need to be replaced.

Chapter

13

Church Going

We went to church in Maine last Sunday, the 21st, and there were fifteen school teachers there. The church is a few miles away in the other Maine town, down the road and north from here. The school in this Maine is two one half miles to the east. I have no idea where all these teachers came from that were in church today but they could sing! It's January and most people don't travel very far this time of year so it really puzzles me. "Rock of Ages" never sounded so good!

The *Wadena Pioneer* newspaper was lying on one of the pews in church. The teachers, I was told later, came from all over Otter Tail County so one of the teachers must have brought the paper along. The *Pioneer* talked about teacher's wages. The paper said that the number of teachers in the area dictates what the wage for each teacher will be. The more teachers in the area, the less their wages will be. The reputation of a teacher makes a difference in pay too. Each teacher needs to pass a county exam, and the qualifications from that exam will decide for some what pay will be. The *Pioneer* said that in order to get a certificate to teach, each teacher needs to score as follows: 65 percent to teach third grade, 75 percent for second grade, and 85 percent for first grade. Also, there are geography and history questions. The ranking after oral answering will be indicated on the certificate. Each year, a Teacher's Roll of Honor" is published about April 1st. Teacher's Exams will be March 10th here in the Maine school because of its central location in the county. I think we have one of the smartest teachers in Otter Tail County in my school! It's a good thing so many of the teachers were at church or there wouldn't have been many there. Many parishioners stayed home, still affected by the grippe.

In another pew was a recent *Weekly*. I read it while Mom and Dad talked to the neighbors and caught up on "the news." Part of the reason we go to church is to hear the local "news." Some call it gossip but we don't. Maine doesn't have a newspaper like the bigger towns have. We have a lady that writes for the paper and sends the news by stage over to the Fergus *Weekly* to be printed in the paper. When we see the paper, it is "old" news. Church gatherings and monthly prohibition meetings are a much better way of finding out what is going on in the area.

My options when they are visiting are to either play with the minister's sons or to find something to read. Since the Anderson boys have a habit of getting in trouble, I choose to read. One of the articles in that paper suggested what to do if someone has the grippe. The article says that persons who have a cold are much more likely to get the grippe. The most critical time, or the time when it spreads most, I guess, is when a person is recovering from the grippe. So many people cough and cough, spreading the germs when they do. A relapse can end in lung fever or pneumonia. I have never understood why it is so important to keep the feet dry and warm. Who'd get their feet wet in the cold? Who wants wet feet at this time of year is beyond me! Dr. Pittitt gives a dose of quinine to a person with the grippe. He says it "keeps up the vitality," whatever that means! Chamberlains Cough Remedy usually promotes a prompt recovery, I know. Chamberlains worked when I had a bad cold, so I suppose it will work for the grippe too. Chamberlains remedy is not sold at McConkey's store. N. J. Marteumen peddles it. Mom got a supply from him last time he came around. He comes more often in the summer but tries to come about every three months, even in the winter if he can get through the snow with his horse and buggy. I've often wondered if he and the Medicine Man ever get together and share *cures*.

Best thing that happened on Sunday after church is that Miss Van Vlect stopped and told me that drawing is "being introduced" into the school curriculum. Miss Van Vlect will go to a *chautauqua* (a meeting for lectures and education held in a building - the topic this time is art) in February and learn the White's New System of Drawing. I can't wait! I love to draw. I hope that I sew enough bags and can save enough to get a new sketch book soon. My old sketch book is full. I suppose I could erase the drawings that I am not happy with and redraw on those pages, but I can't ever seem to get all the pencil markings off the paper. Besides, I would have a hard time choosing which sketches to erase. Each sketch is usually a memory of something that I don't want to lose. In each sketch, I have drawn my version (memory) of what happened.

Mom had some of her cough syrup with her at church to give to friends who were suffering from the barking cough (grippe) that is going around. I hope the minister doesn't taste it or she will be kicked out of the temperance group and probably church too! The cough syrup is made from equal parts of honey, lemon juice and whiskey. We don't drink at our house. The syrup is considered medicine, but I am not convinced that either the

70

minister or the temperance ladies would agree. It soothes the throat and stops the coughing for a while, especially if it is warmed when taken.

Mom sat in church by Mrs. Andy Wallace who had her arm in a sling. She was fretting something awful! Dr. Pittitt set the arm Mrs. Wallace dislocated at the elbow when she drove off the road's edge, tipping the cutter, on her way to the Pember's party. The Jones family, who were also headed to the party, came by and found her under the cutter. Mr. Jones pulled the cutter off her and helped her into their wagon. Mrs. Wallace was a little dizzy, we were told, when she first got into their wagon. The cutter was smashed but the horse was fine. When they got to the party, Dr. Pittitt was there and fixed her up. The Jones family took her home afterwards.

The Pembers must have had some party! Mosher talked about the beautiful dinner the next day at the mill. He usually doesn't gossip so it must have been really something! The Pembers invited some guests for dinner *and* supper. Others were invited just for supper and the dancing that followed. The Pembers live close to Perham which is north of church about eighteen miles. Mom and Dad weren't invited. The only contact we as a family have with the Pembers is at church so none of us know them very well.

I heard Mrs. Thomas say when she came to talk to Mom about a sick neighbor that a prohibition meeting was held last night at the schoolhouse by us. Mr. J. Allen of Girard and Mr. Mosher came and delivered "rip roaring" messages to the few people who were there. Thomas said many usual attendees stayed home because the grippe has really affected so many. We kids wonder when school will start again. I hope it isn't soon. Ross and I are having too much fun fishing through the ice on Lake Leon to the south of our homestead. The ice is very thick at this time because it has been so cold. It is safe for us to fish there, much safer to walk on than it was when Little Wolf fell

71

through the ice.   Ross and I caught five frying pan size crappies yesterday. It was Ross' turn to take the fish home for supper. I helped clean them before they froze. I expect the next time I see Mrs. Barry I'll get a great big bear hug. She won't clean fish but will fix them anytime if they are brought home to her cleaned.

I overheard someone say today as I left for home after delivering meals to the men in line at the Maine Mill that there is a new mill, the Red River Roller Mill, operating in the area by a man named J. H. Featherston. In an advertisement in the *Weekly* he is offering a trial grain grinding in order to stir up business. The *Fergus Weekly* also had an advertisement for the Maine Roller Mills, the one run by Mr. Thomas near us. I told Mom that she needed to get busy and have lots of food ready. The story written about Thomas' mill said that its "capacity has been doubled" and that the flour made is "better than ever." I knew that he had enlarged the mill but I didn't think that it was able to grind double of what it first could. Everybody knows that we have the best miller in the state. Dad is thinking about raising rye and buckwheat because Thomas is looking for those kinds of grains and will pay more money for them per bushel. The advertisement says that there is a free barn for the animals by the Farmer's Roost. I know because I stopped there last night that the Roost and the free barn in the advertisement are both full. Men have been around asking the homesteaders close by if they have any rooms to hire. Most mornings when I don't have school, knowing the mill is very busy now, I go down there to see if I can earn any pennies.

Yesterday when I was down by the mill, I wandered over to the store. Mr. McConkey was unpacking a new shipment that the stage brought earlier in the day. I love the smells of the fresh spices and tobacco. Mr. McConkey is not well so I try and help him with the lugging as much as I can. For that help he usually gives me three licorice sticks which I love. When there is nothing for me to do, I try and sit in the corner by the big barrel stove and eavesdrop. Mr. Henry was there from Battle Lake and said Logan will soon be in town. Logan is the huge Clydesdale horse that stands at stud. Our Belgians are big but this horse is supposed to be much bigger. Sitting at the store and *listening* to the "news" is always better than reading the newspaper.

Chapter

14

Reading and dreaming

It's the middle of February and the snow is almost gone! I can't believe it! It was 59 degrees out today! The thaw isn't helping us get the logs out of the woods for the new house. The ground is still frozen out to the woods where the logs are, but the roads and ruts are full of water from the thaw and the traffic to and from the mill each day. The sleigh is of no use nor is the sled, making the logs impossible to load. When Dad and I are out in the woods, I usually have something to read with me to pass the time. While Dad cuts the huge tree down, I read until it is time to lug the branches he cuts off to the burning pile.

I wish I could use the Fergus Falls School reading room. The last *Weekly* said books were bought and a room was set aside in the school. According to the *Weekly*, the room is open Saturdays. I'd like to be able to look at Frank Leslie's *Illustrated Newspaper, Harpers' Young People,* the *Popular Science Monthly*, and other books that were listed available. I saw a *Popular Science Monthly* at Grandpa's last year.

I have an idea for a feed bag for horses that I saw mentioned in the *Monthly*. I am sure it would sell to the men who come with their wagons full of grain for grinding. Dad makes money doing carpentry work. I'd like to find something to make money at too. I showed Mom the feed bag drawing and she thought it was a good idea too. Looks pretty simple to make. I told Mom if she would help me make the cloth part, I would get the hides to make the straps. We could make lots of money selling the bag to the people who come to grind grain. Feeding the animals that bring the wagons would be much easier, and they could use some of the feed from the mill store.

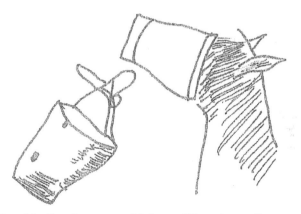

Maybe McConkey would be willing to sell some of the feedbags at the store for us. He has other items in the store "on consignment" he calls it. They give him a percentage of the total cost of the item for being able to have it in his store for sale.

In the last *Weekly*, there was an advertisement for "Free Educations for Girls." Nise is excited! The advertisement says that the *Ladies Home Journal* will provide a "complete education" for $1.00 for a full year's study. Girls have to be 16 years old. Mom pointed out that Nise would have to get 1000 subscribers for the *Ladies Home Journal* at a cost of $1.00 per year. I don't think there are that many people in Otter Tail County! She isn't quite sixteen yet, either, Mom reminded her. Nise would rather be a teacher than a nurse. She can't imagine nor can I working at a place like the State Hospital for the insane in Fergus. If she knew she could work for Dr. Pittitt, our family doctor, nursing would be fine.

I like Dr. Pittitt. He's a good doctor. When I was at the mill yesterday, I heard someone say that Mrs. Patrick Moore is very sick. She has been trying some new electrical appliances with very little benefit. I wonder how she is hooked to these electrical contraptions. To use a contraption, she needs to go twice a week to her sister's in Fergus Falls who has electricity. When I get a chance to look at some of those magazines like the *Popular Science Monthly,* I am amazed what contraptions some people will connect to their bodies, hoping to get well. None of us here around Maine have ever seen one of these contraptions that she talks about. No one that I know of has electricity yet either. We all still use candles or an oil lamp.

Dr. Pittitt sees Mr. Blaisdell weekly too, trying new medicines he hears about for the mentally insane. No one knows what sets off Blaisdell's bouts of anger and wandering. Most times when Blaisdell has one of his spells, he walks out of the house with his ax, heads towards the woods, coming back empty handed. At lease he doesn't rant and rave like Maria does when she is petitioning congressmen for more pension money. I have suspected for a long time that Mr. Blaisdell isn't as "sick" as he plays. Once he winked at me as he hiked off to the woods, almost telling me that I need not worry, that he wouldn't harm anyone. It sort of seemed that way too when Little Wolf fell in the lake. I know I've said this before

– I bet it is his way of getting out of work! Who wants to hire someone insane? This way he and his wife get free meals and a room whenever he is committed for a time at the insane hospital at Fergus. He gets a room because he is a patient and she gets a room because she is caring for him. Quite the deal, I think.

The town board met and decided that the road situation due to the new mill needs repair. Dad and I couldn't agree more. The logs we bring out of the woods almost roll off the wagon because the road is so bumpy. One day, the whole stack cut loose. It is a good thing there were two wagons behind us. Those fellows had no choice but to help Dad if they wanted to get to the mill. I'm not strong enough to lift those logs; that's for sure! With the early thaw and the number of farmers that are coming to grind their grain to flour, something must be done. The town board is busy laying out a plan for the new roads leading in to Maine and the mill from all directions.

Before supper, I ran down to the mill to see if Ross might be there. He'd been there earlier, I guess. Mr. Adley came to the mill today and said that his wife is recovering from a black eye she got when her runaway horse took her for a ride in the cart she was driving. I can just see her flying down the lane, screaming for help and frightening the horse more. It's a wonder that a black eye is all she got from the ordeal. Adley also said that F. M. Mosher lost a good horse this week. Seems Mosher's horse fell on the slippery wet ice from the thawing and hurt its spine, having to be destroyed because it couldn't walk well from the fall. I hate the thought of a suffering horse! Horses are temperamental creatures. If you talk to them nicely, they will do what you want. If they sense that you are scared or not in control, they will do what *they* want and there isn't much you can do about it. Mrs. Adley found out the hard way, I think.

Maine was full of people yesterday. Mr. McConkey had an auction in hopes of closing his store. He has not

77

been well and has had to close the store at times because of his illness. His last sale amounted to $1000, but McConkey says it will be a while before he is able to close out his stock. The *Weekly* says that he "still has about $3000 worth left in his store. In spite of the sale, he has decided to order in the staple goods and keep the store running through the summer at least." I'm glad. I'd like to work there some day. Where else would I get fishing hooks and line to go fishing by the dam if he closed? Those are real necessities for me. There are so many snags around the dam that I lose bait and tackle all the time. The weather has changed, so I am not sure how much longer I can fish by the dam. Right now, ice is not a problem.

Dad and I are woodcutting now that the weather has turned. We are working hard to get the logs and lumber for the house. If we can, Dad wants to cut enough for a barn too. The animals are in a lean-to made with 1 x 4 inch boards but that is only temporary. Eventually, we will have a bigger barn with more stanchions, four walls and a door. We need to get all of Dad's tools inside so they don't rust. The grain storage bins need to be inside and out of the threat of weather too.

When Dad and I came out last to the woods on our homestead, we ran into Mr. Blaisdell wandering around again. He had his ax with him but didn't come over to talk. I will have to go tell Mrs. Blaisdell that we saw him when we get this next load home. Mrs. Blaisdell has trouble keeping track of him. Dad and I were able to bring the six-foot lengths home on the sledge and stand them up in the lean-to away from weather to dry.

The ice on Lake Leon and sloughs around is firm and safe to take the sledge with the weight of the lumber and the horses across and home, making the trip much shorter for us. We piled together the fourteen foot tamarack logs that Dad needs to cut and split into seven foot lengths for fence posts, or the poundmaster from town will be after us for letting our animals roam. Those ewes were at it again! They broke through the wire fence last night, and I had to go round them up this morning before we came out to cut logs.

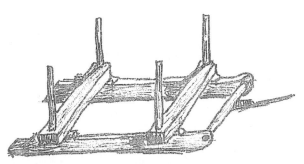

I was warned by the poundmaster when he saw me with the sheep that he would fine us next time he saw them in town. Last summer Grandpa John and Dad cut and peeled more than five hundred aspen for twelve foot long rails. Those have to be hauled sometime soon back to the homestead. It seems like we are always cutting trees for something. With Dad becoming known as a good carpenter and being asked to make furniture as well as chicken coops, he needs wood ready. Our woods needs thinning so it all works out. We are glad each day we can get a load of logs skidded home.

The February thaw we had earlier melted most of the inch thick rim frost that built on the window panes in the soddy. Most of the moisture ran down the walls and soaked the floor, making a real mess for Mom. She decided not to recover the area under the windows that got wet and stained with new muslin, knowing we are moving in the Spring once the new house is built. It's good to be able to see outside through the frost free windows once again.

We almost lost Dad today in the woods! When Dad and I came into the clearing where we cut trees, without realizing it Dad got between a big sow bear and her cubs. She was on the ground and the cubs were in a tree. When Dad saw her, he began waving his arms to be bigger than he is (which is pretty big because Dad is very tall). The bear stood on her hind legs and woofed. Her cubs came barreling out of the tree close to Dad and took off. The sow bear was not far behind them, all running back into the woods by leaps and bounds. When it was over, I shook and shook. I have never been so scared! Dad has me standing guard now when we are in the woods working so that the same thing doesn't happen again. That means I get less reading done but I'd rather have a "whole" Dad than one attacked by a *big* she bear! We have a gun with us if we need it, usually close to me so I can grab it if I need to.

When we got home, we told Mom what had happened and she just shook her head, going over and hugging Dad. After the shock wore off for Mom, she told us Barry dropped the latest *Weekly* newspapers at our house. One "Maine" news article states that the Fergus Falls Flour Mills is running about 6 hours a day. The mill is having trouble with the ice by the dam in Fergus. When they cut the ice away from the dam, the water runs more, and the mill turns better because the water in the spillway is higher. The article in the paper said that keeping the Fergus dam free of ice is more than a one-man task these days with the freezing and thawing due to the recent temperatures.

One of the other papers in the batch he brought, the February 13th *Weekly,* had an advertisement to "buy artificial teeth at Dr. Phalon's" for "$10 per set." His office is over Levi's Clothing Store in Fergus Falls. Levi's is the clothing store that we go to when Mom decides I need a new pair of shoes. Those artificial teeth must be like the teeth that Abraham Lincoln had. Lincoln's were wood. I wonder what Phalon's teeth are made of.

While Dad and I were out in the woods, Mom made some cough drops. Murphy got wet, playing in the snow yesterday, and woke up coughing. I smelled the herbs as we came in the door. Anytime I smell herbs in the house, know Mom is either fixing some game we have shot for supper or is making some kind of medicine. To make the cough drops, Mom uses two teaspoons each of thyme, rosemary and anise in two cups water. She simmers this about 30 minutes and strains this mixture using cheesecloth. Next, Mom adds two cups brown sugar to the liquid and boils it until the mixture forms a hard ball in cold water. Once this happens, Mom pours the mixture into a buttered pan and cuts the slab into small square pieces before it sets too hard. Each piece is rolled in powdered sugar and stored in a sealed jar so moisture doesn't get in and make a sticky mess of the whole lot. The herbs help stop the coughing and smooth out the tickle in the throat. Mom usually has a "fair share" of herbs around from those we are able to pick around here and dry. Others she gets from the Medicine man when he comes through every three months or so. McConkey doesn't carry much in herbs, so we have to rely on these other two sources for what we need. The grippe is still around and we don't want to get really sick since we have been able to stay well this long.

Chapter

15

Soon Spring Time

The March 6th paper that I found in the church pew Sunday had a Fergus Falls seed store advertisement for buying peas and beans from the farmers that grow these as a crop. Reeves Store will pay $20 - $30 per acre for growing them. I told Dad to check at Reeves Seed Store next time he was in Fergus. Reeves is in the Shoemaker building on Lincoln Avenue. This same paper also had a letter to the editor praising the Maine Roller Mills for the fine flour it grinds. The reputation of Ezra Adams, our miller, has spread all over the county. We are so lucky to have him here in Maine. Lots of other mills around would like to hire Adams, but he is content to work for Mr. Thomas. Thomas and his wife are easy to work for if a person gives a "full day's work" for the pay.

Mom sent me to the store after some rye flour to make rye bread. I ran into Ross at the mill and he told me to go check out the school notice on the bulletin board at the store. Usually I am happy with no school but this time I can't wait to get back to the school library. A notice from the *Weekly* hung in McConkey's that school will start again Monday. The article in the paper said that the traveling library has arrived at school. I am going to ask Dad if Nise and I can go Saturday evening and see what books are there. There's enough snow so we should be able to take the horse and cutter. School will only be open an hour from seven to eight that night, so even if it is cold or snowy, we should be all right. The moon is close to full so it will light our way. I hope that with all the people in town grinding grain, we can still go. The roads are crowded these days with lots of people coming and going from town.

There are men always looking for meals when the mill gets behind on grinding like it has been recently. According to the newspaper, Mrs. Wm Spendlove over in Fergus gets $3.00 a week for 21 meals and a room. I told Mom, according to this news story, she could charge more for the meals that she provides and sells to the farmers who stay at the Roost while waiting for their turn to get their grain ground into flour. Some of the farmers have come to the mill often enough now and know that Mom is a good cook. Those farmers waiting will come over to me when I am around, hand me three pennies and ask me to go home to get dinner or supper for them. Mom's pails are filled full with a hunk of meat sliced for a sandwich, a hunk of cheese, four thick slices of her good homemade bread, two or three cookies depending on their size, a piece of jerky, and a piece of fruit, if McConkey has had fruit for sale. I've been shown the sacks that are meals made by some of the other farmers' wives here in the area who also sell meals to these waiting farmers. I know why Mom gets the business. The sacks of food the other women make and sell cost more with less food in them. When I bring the meal back, the farmer usually gives me a copper penny for my running. Mom lets me hang around as much as I can when I don't have to help Dad with the chores, the building, the carpentry, the hunting for our food, or deliver lunches, go to school, or help with the farm in some other way. Most of my day is busy around home. I sneak off when I can, even if it is for just a little while.

The March 27th's *Weekly* that I found at the Roost has a drawing of a beef carcass and the cuts that come from an animal. I brought the paper home from the mill and showed Mom, so the next time we shoot a deer, maybe we can cut it up using the pattern in the newspaper. I remember Grandma Anne talking about the first time she had to help with the butchering. Her story goes like this:

Grandma Anne had never butchered an animal before. She didn't know what to expect. She and Grandpa, carrying his gun, went out to the pig pen. It was time to butcher a pig. Grandpa made sure there was a clean bucket for the blood and instructed Grandma to stir as hard as she could when the blood came into the pail so it would not clot. Grandpa took aim with his gun, shot the pig, grabbed it by the snout and slit its throat. He grabbed the hind legs, lifting it up in the air so that the blood would run out into the pail. Grandma stirred as she was told, as fast as she could. The pig was smaller and younger than most Grandpa usually butchered, but he knew he would have all he could do to lift this one alone. There was no one else close by to help him lift the pig up, so that is why this lighter weight pig was chosen.

Once the blood was done running into the pail, Grandma said she took off lickety-split for their soddy. She had the casings, flour and sidepork bits ready to make blood sausage. While Grandpa was getting the carcass onto a makeshift bench he had made for slaughtering animals, Grandma got the mixture ready, stuffed the casings with the blood sausage mixture, sewed the casings shut and boiled them in a large pot of water. Once they were done, she took them out to cool. Grandma got done just in time to help Grandpa scald the carcass to remove

84

the bristles on the skin. It was a messy, sloppy, job and they were using boiling water besides, so they had to be careful not to get themselves scalded too. The two of them quickly scraped and rinsed, scraped and rinsed until the carcass' bristles were gone. Next, it was time to cut up the animal.

The head came off first. Grandpa cut very deep – all around – and then twisted it off, setting the head aside so Grandma could make headcheese from it later. Next, Grandpa made a delicate cut down through the belly, being careful not to cut the lining that held the guts. Some of the intestines were sorted out to be casings for the sausages to be made. Grandma's big bread pan came in handy to catch the guts as Grandpa rolled the pig over on its side, enough to roll out the guts.

Once the guts were out, Grandpa cut the carcass in half lengthwise and then readied the pieces to be salted down in a brine. He had put another barrel of clean water on the fireplace grate to boil while they were scraping. When the water in the barrel began to boil, he asked Grandma for an egg. She thought he was hungry again or something! It turns out he put the egg into the barrel to test the strength of the brine. If the egg floats, the brine is salty enough for packing down pork. The first egg sank so they added more salt, stirring the water until the salt dissolved. It took three eggs and *lots* more salt until the brine was ready. When the brine finally was ready, Grandpa threw the parts he wanted to salt down into the barrel. The feet they kept out so Grandma could make pickled pigs' feet.

Grandpa watched the pot of brine simmering until he felt the pieces were cooked. Once cooked, he left the meat to sit in the brine and cool overnight. Grandma "called it quits" for one day. She was tired. Grandpa laid out the best cuts of remaining meat that was not "salted" to freeze overnight on the snow which he protected by a clean piece of canvas with boards laid over so no animal could carry off the pieces. The head and feet were brought in to the soddy and put in the coldest part of the house until morning.

First thing in the morning, even before chores, Grandpa took the pig's head and split it with an ax. The brains were pulled into a pile in one of Grandma's big mixing bowls. She had a frying pan with grease heating on the stove, ready to fry the brains as breakfast for her and Grandpa once the chores were done. Fried brains and eggs with toast were one of Grandpa's favorite breakfast dishes. The rest of the head was placed in a large pot to boil. After chores, Grandpa took the meat out of the brine where it had been all night and brought the meat to the smokehouse, hanging each piece in the ceiling. A fire was started in the fireplace to begin the smoking process.

Breakfast that morning was special for Grandpa, bringing back memories of "home cooking" from the "Old Country." Once done with breakfast, it was time to make headcheese. The head was so thoroughly cooked that the meat fell off the bones. Grandpa John took a clean knife and chopped the bigger meat pieces as they were removed from the simmering water into bite size pieces needed for the headcheese. Grandma added pepper and salt. Once they had what they thought was the right mixture, it was dumped into two large baking pans, filling them only half way. On top of this meat mixture, Grandpa placed a board he had cut to fit inside each pan. On all boards, Grandma lay heavy wood-cutting wedges she had boiled clean the day before. They weighted down the boards, causing the fat to rise above the board. As the meat mixture cooled, this fat could be skimmed or scraped away. Grandpa carried the pans out to a makeshift icebox he fixed from some extra sod pieces and a wood door by the side of the house. Grandma used this headcheese as sandwich meat.

The stories Grandpa and Grandma told me always made me smile. The news Mr. Thomas brought early this

86

morning while Dad and I were doing chores made me cry when Mom told me. Mellie, McConkey's nine year old boy and one of my best friends, died at 10 AM today, March 30th. Dr. McLean from Fergus, Dr. Pittitt and two professional nurses Dr. McLean brought with him were with Mellie most of the last three days. I knew he was sick, but I didn't realize how sick he really was. He had lung and brain trouble, which baffled the physicians from the start. He was sick only six days. I lost a real friend today. At times when I went to McConkey's store, I would play with Mellie. Sometimes we put puzzles together. Other times we would read one of the newest books that Mellie had ordered and was delivered by stage. We both like to read and spent time doing just that, reading on the bank by the mill or in my fort. He and I used to fish at the dam by the spillway too. I will miss him.

Grandpa John always says that for each person that dies in this world there is someone born to replace him. Sure enough, the Moshers had a new baby boy today, April 2nd, weighing only 2 ½ pounds! I can't imagine such a small baby. I know yesterday was April Fools Day. I hope Benjamin and Alice Mosher aren't fooled by his small size. They need to be very careful that he doesn't get sick. I am told that they have to feed him every two hours or so, hoping he will gain weight fast.

Mr. Blaisdell must have known it was April Fool's Day yesterday too. He was out wandering again. Nobody knows for sure if he is truly crazy or if he is just a prankster and likes to trick people. He has never harmed anyone but he has done lots of little things that don't seem quite "normal." He was seen over in the church graveyard in Maine north of here. Mrs. Anderson, the minister's wife, watched him from the parsonage kitchen window. Why she was looking out her window at 2 AM, I am not sure. She saw him run behind a large tombstone, sit there in hiding a bit and then jump up, yelling "April Fool! April Fool!" as loud as he could. He ran to the next largest stone nearby and did the same thing! Watching him jump and yell four or five times in a row, she decided to wake her husband and tell him. Reverend Anderson got dressed, went out, got Blaisdell in their cutter and drove him home. When Reverend came home, he told his wife that Blaisdell had a "strange smell about him, probably from too much cough medicine" he thought! I bet he had been boozing and that is why he was so whacky in the graveyard.

Someone toppled the poundmaster's outhouse last night as an April Fool's prank. He was at the mill asking if anyone knew anything about it when I went there this morning to see if I could help. Was he mad! Good thing we built that fence and the ewes are penned up these days or he would be blaming me for toppling the outhouse, even if I am not strong enough to do it. I'd bet Reverend Anderson's boys were up to no good again. They are always plotting something. I'm glad we live in *this* Maine, and not in the *other* Maine where the minister and his family live. Who knows, maybe our outhouse would have been tipped over too by those rascals!

Chapter
16

"Minnesota Blizzard" visits Maine

Each day we are here has some different excitement. Mr. Blaisdell's April Fool's prank was the last straw for Mrs. Blaisdell. She took him to Fergus Falls to the insane asylum today. I hear the law says the asylum superintendent has the authority to admit a person or not. Mrs. Blaisdell intended to stay there and care for her husband. She had done this once before when he was committed under the old superintendent who moved down to the Willmar State Asylum. The new superintendent objected to her staying. This superintendent did not want the government to have to pay for her food and room even if she was helping care for her husband, so she brought Blaisdell home here again. The superintendent won't admit Blaisdell until he does something violent. Wandering the woods with an ax in his hand isn't a good enough reason, I guess. Maybe the superintendent didn't want to have Mrs. Blaisdell nosing around the asylum, watching how the inmates are treated. The Blaisdells just got home when the stage came to town from the opposite direction. On it was the "Minnesota Blizzard," Blasdell's sister, Maria.

Maria is quite the character! When she was last in Washington D.C. trying to get pension money, she went to church there. The church she chose to visit was a new form of religion started by two La Due brothers. Maria wore her beautiful blue, shiny silk dress and hat that day. Trouble was that one of the beliefs of this group was plainness of dress. She stuck out like a sore thumb! This group believed that simple clothing meant you got salvation. In their eyes, she was really wicked! All jewelry or gaudy decorations on clothing were forbidden. Wouldn't you know it! She had worn her best pearls with long dangling earrings too. During the service the singing got so spirited that Maria moved away from the stove, fearing it would shake off its feet, starting a fire. Another of the religious beliefs of this group is that all dreams are God speaking to the person and should be acted on immediately.

The reason she came to visit her brother is because she had a dream one night while she was in Washington. Her dream was about her brother and his land here in Maine. In her dream, at the center of a hill at the backside of his forty she was shown a pot of gold. She told the Blaisdells in no uncertain terms that God revealed to her where this pot of gold was. As soon as she was off the stage, setting her travel bag in the soddy, Maria ordered her brother to find a sturdy shovel and follow her. She began to walk through the woods to the back of their homestead where there was a small hill. Blaisdell, ax and shovel in hand, followed her to the hill which was about a hundred yards from a creek that fed through the property. Once at the spot, she ordered him to dig. Dig he did, finding nothing but rocks and roots. Well past noontime, both of them were hungry so they trudged back to the soddy where Mrs. Blaisdell had dinner ready. After eating, the two of them tore out again to the spot, but this time Maria ordered Blaisdell to bring a hand cart along to haul the gold back. She was sure they were close to the pot of gold. Blaisdell dug and dug again huffing and puffing from the exercise. The hole got deeper and bigger. When he was tired, Maria dug until her small, soft hands were all blistered. The two argued about continuing on this venture. Maria's begging, sure that her dream was a vision from God, got Blaisdell to dig some more.

Supper time came and he was bone tired, so Blaisdell handed Maria the shovel, told her to do what she wanted, picked up his ax and left for home. She ranted and raved for a while until she realized he was not going to dig any more and marched back to the house behind him. A neighbor saw the two as they came back, each looking wilder than the other. Blaisdell carried his ax and Maria pushed the cart, her long hair once in a bun flying in the wind loosened from all her digging, hurrying behind screaming her lungs out! To this day, there is a deep hole on the back on Blaisdell's forty. No gold was ever found. The church she started over at Pelican in one of the empty sod houses stands vacant today too.

Mom spends as much time as she can these days dreaming and it has nothing to do with that church! She is busy mapping out her garden plot. She bought seed before we came, not knowing what would be available in the new area. Mom does not like to barter for seeds as some do when coming to a new area, mostly because she is particular about what kind of vegetables she plants. She is careful, planting only those seeds that have given a good yield other years. Now that we are here, we find we didn't need to bring all the things we did, including garden seeds. McConkey's store has a good supply of most things and

Fergus is not that far away when something special is needed.

Mom enjoys cooking too much not to have the vegetables on hand to use, so it is important to her to get the garden in as early as possible We will plant early potatoes, cabbage, brussels sprouts, carrots, rutabagas, beets, beans and peas to store, and cucumbers for pickling – all marked on her planting plot. Mom and Dad plant the potatoes first. He goes ahead making the rows for the potatoes they cut up the night before. Each potato has to have an "eye", the place where the piece will begin rooting. Mom drops the potato pieces in the evenly spaced holes and rows. Dad covers each one and stomps it down. A week or two later, we plant the rutabagas, carrots and peas. Beans and some of the other seeds will be planted closer to the first of June. Sometimes we pay attention to when the full moon comes and sometimes not, depending on the time of the month it is due. Mom brought flower seeds too. I wonder if she will plant them this year or will wait until the log house is built.

A good gardener plans space well. While Mom is thinking about her garden plot, she usually does some sewing or mending. Those ewes I herded all the way here on the trail are finally useful! Grandma Anne gave Mom some wool ready to card. Mom is twining together some of the wool from the shearing of the cantankerous ewes we brought, combining it with the wool Grandma gave her. During the evening before bed, Mom sits with the cards, working to get the wool ready to spin. When she has another idea for the garden, she writes it down and continues to card. The sound of the spinning wheel is a comforting sound with its whirring as she takes the carded wool and twists it to make the fine yarn to knit. I've outgrown my socks again so Mom needs to card and spin so she can knit me a new pair or two. I am getting blisters on my feet where the holes in the socks are. Most of the summer, I don't wear shoes unless I'm "working."

I wandered out today since there was no school because of the teacher testing and discovered McConkey is having a sale again. Mom wonders if he is trying to sell out again. She took the horse and cart to town after I came home to watch Murphy and bought 14 pounds of sugar for $1.00, 12 pounds of cut loaf sugar for the lunches she packs for $1.00, 20 pounds of rolled oats for oatmeal in the morning for $1.00, five pounds of cornstarch for 15 cents along with 10 pounds of coffee for $2.00. She also bought some toweling that usually costs 12 cents for nine cents a yard. She uses the toweling to wrap some of the lunches and dinners she packs for the men at the Roost if they don't have a pail to pack with them. Mom spent quite a sum of her stash of money she has saved from making those lunches, but she can spot a good deal at any store and tries to take advantage of them when she can.

McConkey's family moved up from the city last week. Maybe he will change his mind about selling out the store now that they are here. Many times when I have been in the store, he talks about family and has been lonesome for them. He suffers from neuralgia according to Dr. Pittitt and has had to close the store some days when he really gets ill. Sometimes he has such severe pains around some of his nerves that he doesn't know what to do with himself. That's when he seems to have another sale. People who know about his bargains have been sending him mail orders, and the good-natured stage driver that comes through picks up the orders and charges the people who order 10 to 25 cents per delivery, depending on the distance. One day the stage driver took $100 worth of orders of various kinds to Fergus. McConkey often sells three dozen clothes pins for five cents! That's cheap! Mom says his spices are really reasonable and very fresh, making her baking taste so good. It will take her a while to get back.   She stops on the way and visits with Mrs. Thomas before she comes home.

With Mom gone, I was busy entertaining Murphy. We were outside and I heard this honking. I got so excited! The geese are back! I saw the great V in the sky, formed by the flocks of cackling geese moving northward. I am sure some will stay in this area. I remember their noise when we stayed at Grandpa and Grandma's last summer. The squawking seemed to continue all night one time when we first got to their place. Later, Murphy asked Dad how the geese knew where to come back to each year. Dad's answer was, "It's one of nature's secrets not yet revealed to man." I told Murphy later that I trained all the geese when no one was looking and Dad didn't know it. This was to be "our" secret – as blood brothers! He believes me! Imagine that!

We had an unexpected visit from three men the night the geese came back. When the men crossed the Red on the corner of our land, they scared the geese and the squawking woke us up. I was so glad I wasn't in the fort, sleeping alone. The men were on their way north to Bemidji to go work in a lumber camp there and needed a place to rest for the night. Dad told them to bed down in the lean-to if they wanted but not to light any fire. In the morning when Dad got up, they were getting ready to leave. Dad brought some bread, jelly and milk for each of them for breakfast before they left again. Each thanked Dad and off they went down the path - north. Later, we found out that these men were probably part of the group that had been in jail.

Last year, the Oriental Limited was held up at Carlisle. After a long court trial, four men were put in jail - three in Fergus and one in Stillwater. The story is that these jailed men were planning to rob a train but not the one at Carlisle. Because they were jailed for something they didn't do, they were set free. Being "in the area," even

94

if you are planning another robbery, isn't "cause for jail time" according to the circuit court judge so they were let go. Dad was glad these men were tired when they came. None of his tools were missing when he checked, so they must have been in a hurry to go north. I wonder if they ever did go work for the lumber camp.

Chapter

17

Time Before Planting

The neighbors tell us that the ground frost has never been out this early in April. We have sloughs on our acreage that were not there when Dad came last year. Since there is no place for this water to run to, we just have to wait until it soaks into the ground. We are told where we have less sandy soil and more "black" soil, the water disappears like magic but leaves behind a quagmire of sticky mud, "hard to cross by man and beast." Our pigs love it! It is hard to keep them from being belly deep in the mud these days.

Since it is too wet to do any field work, Dad and I, when I don't have school, are spending time in the woods again. The wood for the house is ready but Dad knows he will need a considerable number of fence posts and rails to mark the planted grain, oats and potatoes on our land. With the favorable weather, Dad asked me to stay home from school two days so we can haul out of the woods what logs are ready. He added these posts and rails to the pile that he and Grandpa John cut and hauled out of the woods last year when the two of them were here before we moved. They cut over a thousand stout twelve-foot rails and split out 350 oak posts, each about seven feet long, three inches thick and eight inches wide. Each post needs a hole chopped and gouged out to receive the ends of the two rails overlapping one another, making a post and rail fence.

The fence will sit two rods out from each field or garden area, giving Dad turning room on all sides of the enclosure for whatever horse and implement he uses. Splitting rail and fence is usually winter work, but Dad wanted to be ready this year for the new crops, knowing that there will be animals both tame and wild roaming around our new forty. Damage to the field and garden would be disastrous for us this early in our settling in this new area. Plus, the wood is *free*. The wire for fencing would be expensive. We could afford the wire but Mom and Dad like to look of the rail fencing defining our land.

The last *Weekly* has an advertisement for 45.30 acres, more or less according to the government survey, of land for sale in Lot 3, section 19, town 133, range 42 for $350. Rumor is that the homestead claim was lost because the person made no improvements within the specified period that the law requires. It has more open land for grain farming than our land does so it is more expensive. Dad and I are going to the courthouse soon to ask where this land is and to look at buying it. Maybe some day that will be my farmstead. For now until I get stronger, Dad will hire out the tillable acreage. Who knows what I will do when I am done with school.

Clearing new land is a slow process. The twenty acres, that Dad plans to use as field for grains that weren't stripped of sod for our house, need to be cleared of brush first. I am not strong enough to handle the plow yet. It has to be in the upright position, lifted on the handles so that the nose of the plowshare is hard against the turf that is to be turned over. Our two horses move on "buck" command, which means to move forward. When the plow takes hold, we yell, "Buck!" Just like magic, they move forward and a black-brown shiny furrow turns up. The sod is so filled with roots and some rock that it will take time to work into a good field. Sometimes the roots are so strong that Dad needs to use an axe to cut them away from the ground. The first outside furrow is always the worst.

The next furrows go faster, each turning over on the other until the area is all dead-furrowed. Dad plans to enlarge the planting plot each year until he gets the twenty acres that are open all ready for planting. When it is all dead-furrowed, Dad will use a drag he fashioned from some aspen and a log chain to smooth out the new broken ground. The stones are another matter. We'll take the cart Dad made one of the early nights we were here in the area from some of the lumber he and Grandpa John had ready for the house. Dad attached the two wheels we brought with us on the schooner. We'll hitch Benji, our paint, to the cart, using it to lug the stones out of the field. Mr. Barry tells us this is not the last time we will pick rock. The ground yields what the homesteaders call "winter potatoes," rock that pushes up through the ground each time the ground freezes. I like potatoes but I don't think I will like this new variety at all!!

So much of May has been rainy that Dad has spent a considerable amount of time woodworking in the lean-to. He made the ladder backed chairs for the house, the seats and flats of the ladder from the basswood, the other parts from oak. Mom has been after him to make a wooden butchering bench of oak with all parts tongue and grooved together, about five feet long and two and one half feet wide. She knows more butchering is ahead and wants a better area to lay the carcass than on two flat sided logs on stumps. Mom wants the table to have a "bowl" shape in the middle so that the dead animal being butchered won't roll off so easily when the table gets slippery from the carcass.

For someone who had never been around animals or butchering, Mom does really well. Even if it bothers her to do the butchering, she never lets on. A week ago, I saw her go out to the hen house, grab one of the older chickens, take it to the wood block outside and cut its head off with an ax. I was pretty proud of her. The first time she saw Dad do this, she ran the other direction, not used to the chicken flopping on the ground as it dies. I knew Mom was sick and tired of this "old cluck." All of us hated to pick her eggs. She was a genuine old "battle axe" type cluck, pecking and fighting when anyone came close to her nest. Dad tried to break this chicken from her pecking habit by dunking her in the water trough one day. Next time we went to pick her eggs, she was meaner than ever. The chicken stew tasted good, knowing I won't be pecked by her any more. Even for me, it is hard not to think about the butchering part, particularly if what I'm eating has been an animal we have had for a while which has become sort of a pet, especially when I am eating the meat from that animal. I try not to get too attached to any of the animals I know will eventually find their way into the stew pot. What I hunt and kill seems different. I can eat that meat without much problem. I suppose that is because I have not seen the game animals daily as I have those we raise from babies born here on the land.

Chapter

18

Adding Stock

It is soon time to get the pigs that another neighbor has promised to us once his sows farrow. Pigpens are something else to build! Dad found somewhere several big-leaf aspen. Off and on all last week, Dad kept very busy, cutting each aspen into four feet long "strips" no more than five inches in diameter at the largest end. These strips Dad sharpened on one end and drove each into the ground about four inches apart, closing in an area about a hundred feet square. Dad placed a feeding trough made from another hollowed out basswood length, close to the corner nearest the soddy and fashioned a sty for easy access into the pen. When Mom has potato peelings or other leftovers we don't eat, she can easily use the sty to cross through the fence to feed the pigs. The pen enclosure contains a number of trees that will be shade in the hot summer days for the pigs.

As luck would have it, when I took the eggs and extra butter off to McConkey's to trade for flour and sugar, I saw the pig farmer today in the store and told him Dad was ready for the pigs. He told me he'd be over tomorrow and he was.

He brought the pigs each in its own gunny sack lying in the back in a small cart. We heard the squawks and squeals of the pigs before the cart came into view. Because the pigs were weaned only three days ago, we'll use some of our leftover winter potatoes, not the rock kind, to cook a mash to feed them.

I was around when Mom made the mash and did it stink! From the cellar, Dad got about a dozen potatoes which Mom scrubbed and cleaned, putting them in her big black cooking kettle. Into that pot Dad dumped two quarts of oats, putting this kettle over an open "eye" of the stove. Some water must have been added but I don't know for sure. Once the pot started to boil and stink from the almost rotten potatoes, I excused myself and went to the barn to see the newborn calf. I stayed there quite a while, knowing that this mixture needed to cook and cool before the potatoes and oats could be mashed together so the pigs could be "slopped!" Nise came along with me, heading to the nearby woods to cut some weeds the farmer told us the pigs love. I guess this fall we will have to gather acorns for them too . . . and the *smell* of pigs is something else we will have to contend with later when it gets hot! I almost forgot how bad pig smell was at Grandpa and Grandma's last summer when the temperature reached 90 degrees and the pen heated up!

While in the lean-to, I looked out towards the woods and noticed the ruffed grouse were drumming again. I remember last year at Grandpa's asking Dad what that same noise was and if it were Indians somewhere in the area. That's when I first learned that the beating of the wings makes the drumming noise. It is part of a mating dance, I guess. The grouse aren't the only ones to disturb

102

our peace these days. The prairie chickens are squawking, the ducks are quacking, the geese are honking and so are all the birds, each looking for a place to nest and raise young. Add to that the croaking of the frogs down by the riverbank along with the endless crows that seem to be in this area! Living in the country isn't always quiet. Neatest of all is to see a bald eagle soaring over Lake Leon or the Red. Dad warned me not to hunt for a while. It is important that the young get raised, so we have them to replace those that we take for food to live on each year.

Unfortunately, the "vampires" are back too! With spring always come the crawling, blood-hungry vampires: the woodticks! Now, any time we are out, we need to search our clothing and our bodies when we come in and squash any woodticks we have carried in with us. Soon the other flying blood-suckers will be here too: mosquitoes. Sometimes the mosquitoes are so bad that we have to stay indoors if the wind is not blowing, especially after dusk. If we have to use the outhouse, we make a beeline for it as fast as we can, shut the door quick, get our business done, and run back as fast as we can.

Since Dad has not had time to spread the manure pile over the fields, we have a fly problem too. Thank goodness the pile is by the lean-to barn. The flies and mosquitoes mean we cannot have our windows open because we do not have any screening on them.

Murphy feels very important these days. It is his job to keep busy with the fly swatter, trying to hold the level of invaders down as much as he can. Mosquitoes are harder for him to "hunt." I know that the Indians smear bear grease on their bodies so they don't get bit so much by the mosquitoes. I don't know which would be worse – to get bit or to try and wash all that grease off. Bear grease stinks too so I guess I will suffer the bites. Good old baking soda that Mom has for cooking works as well as anything on the bites. I mix a little of it and some water into a thick paste, rub it on the bite and let it dry. Usually the itch is gone fairly quickly. Sometimes, lots of swimming in the Red works to stop the itching.

Chapter

19

Census Count

The stagecoach brought copies of the Fergus Falls *Weekly* here. The driver knows the townspeople are interested in the census information. Lots of the townspeople are very stirred up, concerned if they will even *know* the answers to the census questions. Many can't read and will have to depend on a friend or a family member to help them when the census taker comes to the door with the form, asking the questions. Two Thousand people have been hired just in Minnesota to help complete the census. It seems hard to believe that there are that many people in the state! The whole United States census must be done by June 2 of this year. I have the list of questions to answer. I think the government is getting nosy but this is what they want to know:

First, of course, is the given Christian (baptismal) name in full. Second is whether a person has been a member of the United States or Confederate military service, or is a widow of such a person. Third, is a person's relationship to the head of the family. Someone living alone in a cabin or in a loft above a store is considered a family. That seems a little strange. Even stranger is that a hotel, prison, hospital, and asylum are each considered a family by the census people. I'm glad I'm not part of one of those families.

Fourth is the skin color, I guess – white, black, mulatto, quadroon, octoroon, Chinese, Japanese, or Indian. Some of those skin colors I have never heard of or seen in this area. Next is the sex, a person's age to the nearest birthday, single, married, widowed, or divorced. Then come the number of children living and dead, place of person's birth, father's birth, mother's birth and the number of years in the United States.

Citizenship questions follow and then profession, trade or occupation. They want to know how many months a person has been unemployed during this year. I wonder why.

School attendance comes next with how many years and to what grade level, along with a person's ability to read, write and speak English. If not English, what language is read and written by a person. Any chronic disease has to be listed by name and length of time a person has had it.

A person is asked if he has a defective mind! Who is going to say yes? I wonder how Mr. Blaisdell will answer this question. He is the head of his family and will be the person expected to answer. The questions that follow are about defective sight, hearing, or speech, whether a person is crippled, maimed or deformed in any way, and then explaining how bad each defect is. Any prison time must be stated on the form and if a person is a homeless child or is a pauper.

The last questions are all about where a person lives. Does the head of the family "hire" (rent) the home or is it owned? Is it mortgaged or owned in full? What does the head of the family do? If that person farms, is what he cultivates "hired" or owned by him or a member of his family? Is the farm free of mortgage? The very last answer to give is a post office address of the owner of the place one now lives.

Those questions don't seem so awful. Some people are so private and hesitate to give anyone they don't know any information about themselves. Seems to me I heard one of the neighbor ladies say she was hired to do the census. It's unusual for a woman to be hired for such a government job. I hope the neighbors are honest when she comes to the door asking personal questions.

Chapter

20

Excitement abounds

We have a new schoolteacher in District 22. I am sad to see Miss Van V. go. Her new beau she met at church farms over in the Dent area, so she is marrying him and moving there to his homestead. The new person is J. A. Gaylord. The parsonage is having a sing along tonight to introduce Gaylord to the community. I'm going, not to sing, but to scope out the new teacher. I want to ask Ross to come with me to help check him out.

Logan is coming back to Maine Wednesday, Thursday and Friday. Logan is a one-half Clydesdale and-half Canadian French seven-year-old horse that weighs 1,650 pounds. Logan is a dark bay with white in his forehead and white hind legs. He is for hire to sire at the cost of a single mare for $11 or two mares for $20. Fred Hanson lives in Battle Lake and owns the horse. Last time they were here, Mr. Hanson let me sit on him. Logan is so gentle for such a big horse. I can walk up to him, pet him on his nose, nuzzle his mane, and he doesn't even move.

Seems like lots of new things are coming to town. The Solomon Hubbard's Cheese Factory started Monday, just southeast of Lake Leon. Mom is happy there will be another source for cheese in Maine. She has had to have the stagecoach driver buy her cheese when McConkey runs out in his store. April is a good time to begin this business. The cows are coming in fresh and farmers have lots of milk to sell. The factory is capable of receiving up to 1700 pounds of milk each day. That amount daily makes about 175 pounds of cheese. I wonder who will start a milk hauling business, going to the homesteads in the area, pick up their milk and bring it to the cheese house. I would think Hubbard would be glad for daily deliveries of the fresh milk. Hubbard and his family are living in the vacated house on the land that belongs to Perry Kysor, unoccupied since Dr. Pittitt's two sisters died over the last two years from scarlet fever. Somehow the Pittitt's got all the germs out and can now re-hire it.

Dad borrowed a large cooking pot from Mom early this morning. It is planting time and Dad decided this year to seed by hand. Taking a stout cord, he tied an end to each of the handles on the pot, leaving enough of a loop to go over his head. With the cord on his right shoulder and the kettle full of seed on his left hip, Dad tilted the mouth forward enough for ready access with his right hand. By deftly grabbing handfuls and by releasing the seed as he swung his arm to the right and to the left, Dad broadcasts a wide swath of seed as he walks. Sowing grain by hand was a skill he had learned well as a kid. Throwing seed this way, Dad produces a remarkable uniformly seeded plot. Dad reserved a two-rod strip across the north end of the oats field for planting potatoes and peas.

Mom sent me to the mill this morning. These days, she is always out of flour. I came running home with news! Maine got a bad reputation two nights ago. Paul Ray recently came to town to work at the Roost for Mr. Thomas. Two young men he did not know and a crowd of others came to the sod house Ray was renting from Thomas, got him out of bed and made him get dressed, telling him he was wanted down at the Adams and Thomas dam (the dam by Thomas' mill), blaming him for stealing a horse. A young man named Henry swore he saw Ray steal the horse. Ray swore he had not been in that part of town because he was working at the Roost during that time. A rope was put around Ray's neck and another around his waist. He was dragged down to the dam and threatened with drowning unless he instantly confessed his crime. Ray at first denied the crime but got so terrified from the crowd's reaction that he confessed, realizing they would drown him if he did not say what they wanted him to say. Once he confessed as they wanted, Henry untied the

110

ropes and warned him to get out of town at once, without going back to the soddy to get his things.

Ray did what they wanted, walking south down the road from Maine. He went down to Grant County where he was able to find work at a feed store in Wendell. The stagecoach driver came today with the Fergus *Weekly,* which had the story of the drowning attempt. Ray's letter, that he brought to County Attorney Houpt, lists the names of many who were in the crowd that threatened to drown him. County Attorney Houpt declared Ray innocent. Ray was able to name people who were in the Roost while he was working during the time that the horse was supposedly stolen. Henry, Clyde and some others who were in on the attempted drowning have "egg on their face" today. I wonder if they really would have drowned him.

Chapter

21

Planting and Picking

Today is the day to plant those potatoes that are already beginning to sprout in the root cellar! According to Mom, this is what happened. Mom found her best paring knife while Dad brought up the full bucket of potatoes. The same kettle that Dad used for seeding wheat became the bucket for the potatoes. Using his pocket knife, Dad helped Mom and they both made sure each section of potato had at least one "eye."

Out to the garden plot they went. Dad made a row and Mom dropped each potato eye about twelve inches apart down the row. Once done, the seed potatoes were covered with the rake and stomped down. Next, Dad made rows for the peas. Mom was right behind him, planting. When Nise and I came home from school, we saw they both were tired so we offered to do as much of the chores as we could that night, especially entertaining Murphy so they could rest.

It was unusual for Mom, but last night she told Nise and me that we would skip school today. The Farmer's Almanac predicted good weather for foraging in the woods, so off we go. We are looking for berries which Mom makes into jelly, preparing more than we need to feed us so she has the makings for all the lunch and dinner pails she sells to the farmers waiting for their turn to grind grain.

The "greening-up" has started on the prairie and in the woods. Dad left two acres unbroken close to the house so Mom has an easier time foraging than most women do looking for food to harvest. I have the Winchester 22 rifle with because we've smelled skunk recently and don't want to get sprayed. Grandpa told me to sneak up on a skunk and shoot it in the guts. He'll die, I guess, but he won't feel the "shot" right away with all his fat around his stomach. Usually he doesn't spray either if he is shot this way. I'm on the lookout, but I am not sure I will hang around long enough to shoot if I see one.

In one corner of this open area close to the house, we have a wild asparagus plot that Mom cherishes. Nise carries a basket that is long and narrow, made just ready for them. I love asparagus made with Mom's white cream sauce and a little butter. Yum!

Milkweed pods are ready to be picked too. The hardest part for Mom to get milkweed ready for use is all the boiling water that she needs. She has two pots going, one larger than the other. The trick is to put the milkweed in a smaller pot, pour boiling water to cover, boil for one minute, pour off the water and start the process again. If she does this "boiling and pouring" three or four times, the bitter taste to the plant comes out. It's important to always use boiling water or the bitterness sets in the plant. Mom says most people use salted water to boil out this bitterness. What is left is a salty plant, not usable for some foods. I like Milkweed pods with black walnuts. Mom uses

113

toasted walnuts, bread crumbs, salt, thyme, basil and black pepper mixed in with the pods, layering this mix in a flat dish to bake. Once when I was younger, a bail to the small pot came loose. The water scalded Mom on her left arm some. That is one of the few times I have seen Mom cry. It was a good thing Dad was close. Nise ran and got him to help. Mom still has the scars today. I'll never forget that day. Man, did she yell – it hurt her so. Uff Da !

Dandelions, fern fronds, and the first mushrooms were easy to find today as we were foraging. Chanterelle and morel mushrooms are harder to spot under the downed leaves. We have to be careful to pick only those kinds. Some mushrooms are poisonous. One time, Murphy helped us. What *he* thought was a good eating mushroom he picked and threw into the pail. Little did he know he picked a very poisonous one that looks similar to another but isn't the right kind. We had to throw away what we already picked, afraid some of the bad mushroom would stick to the good ones and make us all sick. My buddy, Wing Eagle, eats many kinds of mushrooms, but the Indians have always known which are safe and which are poisonous.

We found lamb's quarters, a green that Mom uses with bacon in a sweet and sour sauce. Some people call this plant pig weed. For some reason, we usually find it along the edge of the fields Dad has cultivated. We gather the whole leaf clusters and the tender stems for use. Tasting much like spinach, and because it "wilts" down when cooked, we picked lots of "quarters." Mom does can a few jars but it isn't as good that way. It gets mushy when canned, just like spinach does. Dad loves bacon so Mom needs to double any recipe she has when bacon is included. I don't especially like the vinegar taste that is part of the "sour" sauce. Adding chives helps cover some of that sourness. Quarters probably will be our supper tonight. We have bacon from one of Bickman's hogs that we bought and butchered. The hams and bacon lengths

114

have hung in our smokehouse once they came out of the salt brine long enough to cure, I think, so they are ready to eat. I love the smell of the smokehouse. The smoke and meat smells mixed make my mouth water.

Frying the bacon mixed with the chives we pick today and boiling up the greens won't take long. When Mom dishes our plates, she crumbles more bacon on top. See why Dad is so happy? Dad calls a dish like this "food from heaven." We only pick enough for a meal. These leaves don't keep, room in our icebox is limited, and they don't dry as well as some greens do for later use. Since Mom plants spinach in the garden, she saves canning shelf room for other things. Lamb's quarters are a once-a-year treat for our family, much like kringle is at Christmas for us. We usually have a couple of suppers when some "green" like lamb's quarters is in season and then it is on to the next "fresh" vegetable we find. I am sure I will be sent out again to do another picking for another supper before the "quarters" turn tough.

Dad has been busy too. The first crop of hay for the animals is ready. It is a good thing Dad brought the scythe when we came in the schooner. He is able to cut about two to three acres a day, swinging the scythe pretty steady all day.

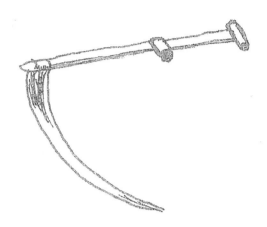

Dad looks so big and his shoulders just ripple when he swings that scythe! I wonder if I'll ever get big enough to swing the scythe. He is tired when the day is done but proud of what he has accomplished.

The big hand rake is used next to gather the hay onto the wagon to bring it back by the lean-to barn for winter use. Dad was happy because he finally got the chance to use the hand rake he made with its back of basswood and its teeth and handle of oak. I wonder if a time will come when Dad will just be a carpenter and hire out our land to someone to raise crops on. Maybe I will be that crop raiser. Who knows!

When I came back from the Red early this morning, I saw that wild onions are sprouting up all over. I can't wait for Mom to make onion pie. She starts with a pie crust and puts in layers of grated sharp cheese from Hubbard's cheese house and the wild onion bulbs. An egg yolk and milk mixture she pours over the onions thickens when baked and turns golden brown. It is yummy, especially when we have a slice of wild turkey breast or a chicken leg with it. We pick as many onions as we can without stripping a patch. Mom wants to make sure that when we come again, there will be more. She pickles the bulbs as a special treat in the lunch pails. See why the farmers at the

Roost want her lunches? Between what Mom has learned from Grandma and the tricks she has learned from the Indians, the Medicine Man, and J. Marteuman, the peddler who comes around when weather allows him to use a horse and buggy, Mom's cooking is tasty, making me want to lick my fingers when I am done eating!

Gathering the greens and things for Mom is one thing. Getting rid of the pests *we* gather is another! When we come back to the house, it is time to pick woodticks off ourselves and each other once again. Mom has us take off our clothes, put them in a pile, and take a bath, making sure that we wash our hair and put on all clean clothes. The clothes we wore are put in a tub of water she has on the stove, ready to use when we come home. The water and lye soap she has in the water kills the critters. We each usually have at least one stuck too. Since we get them off so soon, the itch never is too bad. It's a baking soda plaster time again to stop that itch! Sometimes we just try to pick the ticks off by hand. We find that if we put alcohol on the ticks, it is easier to remove them. One time, some of our neighbors got very sick from tick bites. The doctors did not have any remedy. Eventually, their sickness left by itself. It just goes to show that medicine doesn't have all the answers yet. I am reminded again of Mellie – I still miss him so. Ross is always busy. The Barry family can do a pile of work everyday because they are so many. Many people hire or trade for their help. Ross always brags how much work he does compared to his older brothers, but I know the truth. He's smaller than I am, even though we are born on the same day. He is the *baby* of the Barry family so he really *talks up* what he does. So many times he ends up with *lumps* on his head from the friendly family fights. One thing I learned a long time ago being the middle child in the family – if I keep my mouth shut and do what I am asked, the other two usually get into trouble: the one because she is the oldest and "should know better" and the other because he is the youngest and "didn't listen!" What really saves me from getting into trouble in our family is that I am out of the house for some reason or other most of the time when the weather is good.

Chapter

22

Foraging "Free" Food

Yesterday, Dad made a coop for Ben Mosher's new chickens that came on the stage, much like the one he made for our chickens when they came. Mosher thought the hinged door on the back was a fine idea and paid Dad extra for the invention. Dad's carpentry is getting well known in the area. He sold two chests of drawers he made from cedar to Mr. Thomas who wanted a special gift for his wife. Sometimes he talks of hiring a hand until I am old enough to handle the harrow and plow with the horse behind. I can handle the horse but I am not strong enough yet to wrestle with the equipment. Some days I want to grow up. Other days I am glad to be able to fish the Red or mill stream when I want. The responsibility of growing up and working is scary, not knowing yet what I want to do for the rest of my life.

Mom got Nise and me up early this morning to pick wild strawberries again. She had the clothes wash water already heating and intended to stay home, so we were warned as we left to be careful and not fight. Mom saw half-ripened strawberries in the woods two days ago when she came home from McConkey's store and sent us after them, knowing they were probably ripe by now. It's Mom's turn to bring coffee treats to church and she wants to make two fresh strawberry pies. It happens every time Mom brings treats! Her treats are the first chosen. Her pie crust is so flaky and good. We have flat baskets to pick into so that those little berries don't get crushed.

We didn't fight but I had to help her get home! When we were picking our last patch, Nise must have disturbed a bee, because it came flying at her and bit her on the upper eyelid. Did she yell! . . *and* did she swell up fast! I helped her and we hurried home as fast as we could. This is another time that the Medicine Man's remedies were good to have around. Mom took one look, went to the cabinet and found a bottle of bicarbonate of soda. She took equal parts of the soda and salt, dissolved in a little warm water, and rubbed it on the swelling, being careful not to get any in the eye. I wanted to laugh because Nise looked so awful but I also felt sorry for her, knowing how a bee sting hurts. It took two days before the swelling was all gone. We were surprised that she didn't get a "black eye" from the ordeal too but she didn't.

Those first berries in May are always so good. I can't wait for the blueberries to ripen later on this summer. They are always under the pine trees because they like to grow in the "rotten" pine needles. I hope McConkey has pectin back on his shelf. Mom said she was out so I am sure I will be sent to the store when we get home. Hope he has gotten licorice in again too. I have earned a few pennies sewing sacks at the mill again.

Nise got scared when we saw Blaisdell in the woods where we were picking just before she got bit by the bee. I told her not to worry. I often wonder how Mrs. Blaisdell gets anything done besides chasing after him when he wanders off with his ax. He smiles and winks at me whenever I go by him. It is like he is telling me that he is "play acting," that I don't have to worry. Sometimes I think he wanders off like this so he won't have to work. I have asked and no one seems to know anything really awful that he has done. He gets blamed for some things but most can't be proven.

I don't mind picking strawberries but weeding the garden I hate! I understand why Nise and I need to do the weeding. We are teaching Murphy but he thinks some of the small shoots like the carrot shoots are weeds. We really have to watch what he is weeding. Without us helping out, neither Mom nor Dad would have any time to relax and Murphy would pick the garden bare!

Most of the farmers including Dad have the wheat crop in the ground. Some have planted rye too. Most are holding off planting the field crops of peas and beans until the middle of May. This has been such a strange year for weather with warm weather in mid winter and the frost that we recently had. Frost is still likely and could stunt the crops more yet. The *Weekly* says that the wheat, which was sown early in our area by broadcasting seeds on high ground and froze in the early frost we had, probably won't recover. That means those farmers will have to spend more money to seed over again, if they can afford to buy more seed. Those who can afford and use the press drill pulled by their horse are luckier. That wheat seems all right. The country needs rain.

Those that have some old wheat left over and don't need it for seed are taking it to Battle Lake to sell and are being paid 88 cents a bushel! That's good money for last year's grain. The old grain is being shipped by railroad to Minneapolis to a mill there, I guess. I can sure learn a lot if I sit quietly at McConkeys' by the woodstove and listen. There's a *big* world out there and I want to learn all I can.

121

Mr. Barry settled with Dad today, paying for the lumber Barry used for the roof last January when Barrys had the fire. There was a lot of figuring going on at our kitchen table over coffee. Dad had a list of what Barry lent us when we first came – straw, feed for the animals, etc. Mr. Barry had a list for rebuilding the roof damaged in the fire last winter. By the time it was all over, they called the slate even, shook hands, thanking each other for being good friends and neighbors. The "slate" starts over, I think, as we start building our log house and will need some of their help. It is better, Dad says, in the long run to trade work for work, no money. That way, both parties can still get work done and not spend the hard earned money.

Chapter

23

Log House Building

With the planting done, Dad started the log home he promised Mom if she would move here. That means I'll see more of Ross. "The Barrys are going to help us with the building," Dad said. "We've cut and cured enough wood without having to buy to replace what Barry used for his roof. My carpentry business has been good so I can afford to either pay them or barter for some help moving logs closer to the shed where I have my tools. With their help, we can move more logs in a day that the two of us can move in a week."

First things first in this building process! Dad and I leveled the area where the log house will stand. We dug away the grass that hadn't been stripped for the sod house. It is important that the bottom logs lay slightly into the earth. On the northwest corner, Dad put a four-by-four foot cellar, about five feet down, for winter root storage.

Digging was easier after the roots were grubbed away because the base earth was sand beneath the sod. That's why the rain soaks away so fast up in this area. For now, Dad intends to cover this hole with basswood planks laid into the ground and flush with the floor, covering the hole on all sides. We really need a trap door to this cellar hole and a wooden floor base also, but Dad will do that later when the house is done. For now, he will make sure that there is a small trap door in the kitchen by the wash stand. He will put a drop down ladder there too so that if there is ever a storm, we can get into the cellar without risking harm by having to go outside into the storm.

Grandpa and Dad had cut and stripped big white pine trees into twenty-four and sixteen-foot logs. The shorter logs that they cut Dad will use on the ends and for the roof. Most of the logs have been peeled and flattened on the top and bottom so that each level of log going up should be about twelve inches of wall. With a square, axe and hand saw, Dad cut dove-tail notches into the wall logs on the ends. As each is placed on the other, they intermesh like fingers do in prayer. Planning for the door and windows was not easy. The two older Barry boys came to help. Mom, Nise and I are not strong enough to lift the logs and it is a two man job. Dad uses a tripod and horses with pike poles. Grandpa showed him a couple ways to raise the heavy logs with less help. He always tells me to stand back because he never knows when the horses may move or the poles may shift off the tripod. Dad had made some dowel pins that he drove down from one log to another to hold each layer in place. As each layer is fit and finished in place, Dad uses a long wooden level to make sure one layer levels off the other. With the walls in place and no sign of bad weather overnight, Dad told the Barry boys to go home, asking them to come back tomorrow to put on the gabled roof. You should have seen Nise smile. She knew that she would see her "friend" she has taken a "shine" to again soon!

The boys came back as promised, and they and Dad put the notched rafters up at a four-foot spacing. This way he knows the roof won't sag from the boards and sod it will hold. Once done, the ends of the house were next, cutting each log to fit until the hole to the peak fills. Since the spaces get smaller to fill as the peak is reached, this part of the building went very fast.

The last thing Dad needs the Barry boys' strength for is to put the door in place. Wrestle with it they did! Getting the heavy door on its hinges was not easy. Finally, it too was in place, swinging open and closed without trouble. Each of the boys worked a twelve-hour day and each was tired from all the lifting, I could tell. Dad paid them, shook their hands and sent them on their way home. Mom was glad to see the progress they made but also glad to see the boys go. She had done nothing but cook twice what we normally eat for two days straight. As I went to bed, Dad reminded me that we had windows to get in tomorrow and a lot of chinking to do. I guess fishing with Ross will have to wait for a while again. Maybe he will show up and help with the chinking.

It was raining when we got up this morning but Dad said we could still get those windows put in place. Once we fed the animals, picked the eggs and milked the cow, we headed for the new house. I was surprised I could lift as much as I did. Each of us took a side and hoisted the window in place. I steadied it while Dad toed the window frame to the logs around it. One window needed a little shimming but the others fit just fine. Last to do was to fill all the "holes" in the walls, the chinking. With it daylight outside, we could easily see where these holes were so both of us took the same "mud" mixture that we used on the soddy and went to work plugging holes. I asked Dad once if he was using his drill behind my back making more holes! It seemed like we weren't getting very far very fast at all, plugging up "daylight" in the walls. When we were done with the walls, I asked how we were going to do the roof and Dad said, "Tomorrow is another day. Let's go and have supper," and we did.

The rain stopped overnight. Once the chores were done and the sun dried the roof some, we mixed more "mud" and headed for the roof. Finding the "holes" was harder now because we were looking down on the roof and not up. It took a few "ups and downs" by both of us until we had everything covered. We rolled tar paper on top, fastened it with pegs and began sodding with that thinner cut sod again. Lug, lug, lug! At this rate I will soon have rippling muscles like Dad's, strong enough to handle the horse and plow. Nise came and helped lug sod; so did Mom. We were all anxious to get done and be able to move in.

Sodding the roof took most of the day but finally the last "brick" was laid. We all stepped back to admire our work, pretty proud of what the five of us could accomplish. Even Murphy hauled "bricks" this last day. Nice and I took turns standing half way up the ladder in order to hand the sod to Dad who would take the piece and lay it in place. Dad looked at us and said, "How about we start the barn tomorrow?" and we all groaned. He was teasing. He was tired too.

What we really did the next day was move. Murphy and I have a bedroom to ourselves now. Dad took the bunks apart and we each have a bed, one on each side of the room. Nise has her own room. It's good not to have to put up with Nise's chatter and all those silly girl things all the time.

Chapter

24

May Arrives

Dad has hurt his back somehow from all the lugging and lifting the last few days. As luck would have it, the Medicine Man, "Dr. Koch," came by earlier this morning. Mom spent about an hour with him, refilling her medicine box. She hadn't re-supplied her "doctor box" since he was here last fall. It was getting very low.

Our Belgians, Lefty and Lena, have some cuts from a patch of prickly bush – I don't know what its real name is – that they got into about a week ago. Koch sold Mom some Magic Liniment. Magic Liniment has gum camphor, turpentine, oil of origanum, and sweet oil in it. All that is missing is the alcohol. The Liniment Mom bought is mixed now to use for the animals. Mom bought two batches so that we can use it on ourselves too when we need it. For us to use it as a liniment, Mom has to add another quart of alcohol and shake it well. We rub this on sore muscles. Oh, it feels good.

Koch had with him the cayenne, port wine and tincture of myrrh that Mom needs to make a gargle for sore throats. We always have on hand (or we can buy it at McConkey's) the sage tea, honey, salt and vinegar that Mom adds to the things she bought from him. I'm glad he had the medicines along. I had a sore throat last month and Mom had run out of some of the makings, so I used another remedy which wasn't half as good as this one.

We are on the road to church and it is raining! Hooray! Today's the 15th of May. It hasn't rained for three weeks. Dad put the cover on the wagon so we won't get soaked before we get there. We only got .25 of an inch of rain so far according to the gauge outside the church, but it seems to us as we are on the road home like the crops sprouted up even while we were in church.

We still have that poundmaster, Mr. Futile, hired by the town board to keep the animals off the town road and out of the neighborhood yards. With the traffic that the mill brings to Maine, he is kept very busy. Cows and a few sheep in the area get out of their fencing. The newly planted grass plots around the houses and the gardens are tempting and bring the animals to town to feast on tender new growth they *think* they can't find close to home. Since some homesteaders are not used to corralling their livestock, reminders and sometimes fines are needed to keep the stock closer to their homesteads. One day recently, Mrs. Thomas looked out her back door and saw a cow eating all her peas – pods, plants and all. Was she unhappy! The poundmaster took the cow to the Roost and tied her there while he tried to find out who owned her. I am sure the farmer had to pay that $100 fine to "bail" her out.

I miss Mellie this time of the year. Late May is when we have always been down at the mill fishing for walleye or northern. He has been my partner each spring since I

128

moved here when the fish run over the dam. I went down alone to fish today, hoping to catch enough to sell to the farmers grinding grain at the mill. They pay me 5 cents a fish, gutted and ready for the frying pan. If I can't sell them to the farmers, I take them home to the smokehouse. Our smokehouse has a huge Northern and three walleye hanging from the ceiling beams right now that Ross and I caught two days ago. Ross isn't the fisherman that Mellie was but goes with me when he can. Mom can always use fish for our meals or for her lunch pails that she sells to the wagon masters waiting for their grain to be ground.

The dreaded potato bugs appeared today! Late May through early June seems to bring them each time we plant potatoes no matter where we live. Nise spotted the black and white striped beetles when she checked to see if the peas were ready to eat. She and I love young pea pods! These little beetles lay large clusters of yellow eggs on the underside of potato leaves, which hatch in about a week. Good thing she checked! Getting rid of them is not easy. We usually hold a small baking pan under the plant leaves and beat these leaves carefully with a flat stick to "beat" off the eggs. We will have to walk the rows daily, for a while, trying to get rid of the pesky things! Whatever eggs fall off into the pan, we burn by dumping the pan contents into the stove. What a pain! I could be doing a hundred things in the woods instead of doing this woman's work! I'm glad Ross isn't watching. He would tease me, all the time refusing to help. He's *above* woman's work! Ha! He is just lucky he knows how far from the older brothers that he has to stay when his mouth runs! Believe me, he has learned the hard way!

Chapter

25

Joys of June

The assessor showed up June 5th. You would think the census just done would be enough for the government. B.B. Mosher is the assessor. Two weeks ago we had another census taker here. She was the lady I heard had gotten the job. Mosher, the assessor, is finding out there is a difference in what he as the assessor is told a local man is worth and what the lady census taker was told. Paying taxes on property seems to devalue the property in the mind of the owner. I walked with him as he left to go to the Barry's. I was on my way out to squirrel hunt when he came.

I don't usually beg but this time I asked Mom if she would make squirrel for me. Mom said she'd fix squirrel if I would bring it back skinned and cleaned. I got lucky! I took my gun to hunt today, shot three squirrels *and* a partridge – Dad loves partridge. I got them all cleaned as

Mom asked and was on my way home when I saw a bunch of asparagus ready for picking. I love cream of asparagus soup and I knew Mom had milk from this morning's milking, so I picked as much as I could carry without damaging the shoots. Mom was late in making supper and was so glad that I found the shoots. Nise helped her clean and cut up the asparagus while I helped her get the squirrels ready for the pot to simmer. The squirrels and partridge will be noon meal tomorrow. Nise sure works hard too, though I would never tell her that. Growing up a boy or girl out here on the prairie doesn't matter. There is still a lot of hard work for all of us to do all day long. I am luckier because I get to go out in the woods and wander around some. Nise usually has to stay pretty close to home. She does know how to shoot a gun and has shot squirrels and rabbits, but she doesn't like to clean them at all.

We buy very little meat. In fact, McConkey has very little meat for sale in his store unless it is dried. Fishing is good all year long at the dam or through the ice on Leon Lake in winter. The large mouth bass love the lily pads by the bridge on the west end of the lake. Only trouble with that is that the line gets tangled in the pads when the bass try to shake the hook. We also run an extra cow to butcher each year, do the same with the pigs and ewes. Kill the chickens that quit laying or the mean ones like that old "cluck" Mom beheaded, replacing them with younger ones. Dad and I hunt deer, moose, elk, bear, ducks, turkeys, squirrel, possum, and geese in season. Some of the meat Mom cans; some we salt in crocks; some we smoke in the smokehouse. The most fun but sometimes the most work is making sausage. We have some special recipes from Grandpa John that he brought with him from the "Old Country" and his cooking days there that we use to make links and rings. Neighbors smile when we take them to the church socials for treats.

We usually try and get four deer each fall (two per person) during season. Dad and I field dress the carcass (take the guts out) and then bring it home, usually tied to a horse. Dad then takes a rope and hangs it in a tree for a day or two to *season*. Once it has hung for a time, Mom and he get the deer down and cut it up. The good cuts of meat like the tenderloin we usually eat fresh. The roasts and other good cuts of meat we either salt down or can, to be used later. The rest of the meat is cut into small squares and put in a large mixing bowl. Once all the meat is cut from the carcass, Mom adds marjoram, thyme, salt and pepper to the meat, stirring well. Out comes the old grinder that we have had forever. Ice water if we have ice or very cold water is added to the mixture and the bowl is stirred again. Sometimes she adds onion, garlic, or cheese. Sometimes Mom adds all three spices. Then, the stuffing begins.

The casings saved from butchering the last hog are retrieved from the salt brine and rinsed in a lot of water to remove all the salt. Once water has been run through the inside of the casing, it is time to stuff the casings full. Rules in our family are that we all help with the stuffing process or we don't get to eat any of the sausage. Each casing is stuffed and tied off with a strong cord. The stuffed casing is put in boiling water for a time to cook the meat. When the meat is sufficiently cooked, each stuffed casing is taken out to the smokehouse and hung above the grate to "cure". Somehow, by the looks of the casing, Dad can tell when the sausage has hung long enough. He takes it away from the grate and hangs it in the rafters at the back of the soddy where the rest of the cured meats all hang until we have it for a meal. The smokehouse is one of my favorite places on the homestead. I could stay in there all day! Dad uses a variety of woods – whatever he can find available – apple, cherry, oak or peach if there is some in the area. It is important to cure meat either by salting or smoking to avoid food poisoning.

Perry Kysor's family will forever remember the date June 24th. Mrs. Kysor, Mathew, Marsh, Mr. Munson and the hired girl all somehow ate some food that had gone bad. Ben Mosher and his son came by late in the day to ask Perry to help him and found the family sick. Mosher understands medicine and went to work, after sending his son for Dr. Pittitt. He forced each to take the syrup of ipecac that the family had in their medicine cabinet. Once the ipecac was taken, each waited 15 minutes and drank as much water as they could drink. Ipecac makes a person vomit up what is in the stomach. Mrs. Kysor ran out of ice for her icebox the day before. It has been hot and most likely something the family ate the night before caused the problem, probably the pork she made for supper. When Dr. Pittitt arrived, he praised Mosher for his quick thinking. Most likely there would have been a death or two had not Mosher come along when he did. It was a good warning for all of us to be more careful with food that is not cured in some way or not put on ice.

I was out in the woods yesterday hunting with my gun for partridge, the first chance I've had since I shot the squirrels. School is closed for the summer. I miss Mellie so. Last year the two of us hunted just as school was out and he shot a young doe. I helped him field dress the doe just like Dad taught me before we carried it home to his house. We were able to hunt the first two days just after school was out if we took young does or a young buck which had very small antlers. The herd needs to be culled. The deer population is so large that they are becoming a nuisance for the farmers in the fields and the wives in their gardens.

I saw scat from an opossum when I came back from the mill so I knew he was around. I started checking up in the trees and sure enough, he was curled up in one. When he saw me, he growled, showing his 50 or so sharp teeth. He looks frightening when he growls, but I know that opossums are usually gentle, unless they are bothered by someone. I think this is the one that has gotten into the chicken coop and eaten some of the eggs. I took aim and shot him. Once on the ground, I waited to see if he would move. This time, he was not "playing possum!" I rolled him over, made sure again that he was dead, took out my knife and gutted him. I picked him up by the tail and started for the house. I am not sure if Mom will want to make him for supper or not. Opossum are really greasy. Yuk! He may become pig food if she doesn't want to make him for us. Pigs eat anything!

On a round-about way home, I came across a June-berry grove. When I saw those ripe berries, I knew Mom would want to make sauce. I filled lunch pail that I had with me with June-berries and headed home to Mom. The dark purple berries make wonderful sweet jam or sauce. Too bad I didn't have a bigger bucket. June-berries are the easiest berry to pick, I think. They grow on stems like grapes do and strip right off like milking a cow when the berries are ripe and ready. I have to make sure I tell Mom that I found a grape vine in bloom too. She will be thrilled. She has missed the June-berry and grape wine Grandma had and served on special occasions when we were staying there.

Mom makes all kinds of jam and jelly for us from berries and other herbs. She is so glad there are apple trees on our homestead that will bear apples this fall if the deer leave the apples alone. Mom uses apple juice in most of her jams and jellies. I watched her make mint jelly this winter. She took apples she bought at McConkey's story since she hadn't brought any canned juice with us when we came in the schooner. She cut them up, put them in a kettle and barely covered them with water. She cooked and stirred this mixture until the apples were soft. Next, she drained off the liquid, being careful not to get any of the pulp in the juice. She had about four cups of juice when she was done straining the mixture. To this she added a cup of mint leaves. She let this come to a boil and let it boil for about five minutes. Then, she added three cups of sugar and a little butter. She boiled that mixture for about ten minutes until a drop of the mix in cold water made a little hard ball. Before she filled the jars she had ready, she skimmed off the top so what was left was a nice clear color. We love to have mint jelly when we have lamb. Besides brains and bacon, I think lamb could be one of Dad's favorites too. Lamb is a bit lower on my list of favorite meats. I could live on wild game, probably because I harvest most of it. Dad is way too busy to do much hunting.

Sometimes Mom uses wine for cooking when she knows the meat is tough. The wine helps to tenderize and give the meat a better color and flavor, especially if it has been in a salt brine. If the temperance people knew Mom made a little wine, she would be scolded by them. Mrs. Blaisdell came to temperance meeting one day with wine smell on her breath. No one blames her because of the constant chasing after her husband that she does almost daily. One of the members couldn't keep still and thought it her *duty* to scold Mrs. Blaisdell so much that Mrs. Blaisdell left crying. Some people think they do no wrong and delight in correcting others.

Chapter

26

Midsummer Events

Maine (our town and not the other one up the road) celebrated the Fourth of July with a big picnic across from the dam in front of Wm. and Nona Thomas' old shanty. Plank tables were set up and a Whosoever Will social was held. Mom brought two of her famous strawberry pies made from those strawberries we find in the woods near our home. Blaisdell came with his ax in hand, sat down by me and told me about a fox den that is in a woodpile on the back forty of his homestead. He wanted to know if I would meet him there tomorrow and the two of us would see if we could get the fox out. I told him I would have to ask Mom and Dad if I could. He winked at me and said he would leave the ax home. This is the first time he has really sat and talked to me (or anyone else that I have ever seen and I see a *lot* wandering around the mill and McConkeys' for any length of time). I have never been fearful of him. He sure is foolin' everyone else. No one else goes near him but he never hangs around any place long enough for anyone to spend time with him either. I still think he is play-acting so he doesn't have to work.

When we got home from the Whosoever Will party, Mom sent Nise to the garden to get new potatoes for supper. It's a good thing Nise had the shovel with her because there was a woodchuck in the potato patch. She gave it a whack with the shovel and came running back hollering so loud I am sure they heard her down by the dam! I decided right then and there not to get in any fights with her again! At least Nise showed him she meant business because she "swung before the run!" I took the gun out and tried to find it but the woodchuck must have wandered off again. I came back, got the shovel, dug the potatoes and promised to keep an eye on the patch. Woodchucks are mean critters, especially when they feel cornered.

As I look out the window, I know it won't be long and that waving gold in the field I see will be flat and black furrowed soon. Grain ripened early this year because we had so little rain. Dad will cut the oats today once the dew is off. Weather has been unpredictable and a driving rain or a hailstorm could shell out the kernels and lodge the straw in the field so it would be difficult to cut and lay straight. Dad would rather take the grain a little early and let it dry in the sheaves than risk the weather. Each swing of Dad's scythe makes a swath of some four feet as Dad moves forward about four inches with each stroke. Each time Dad swings, he cuts a width of grain and also sweeps the cutting to the left side of him into a neat row with the heads of the grain forward. Slow and steady . . . slow and steady . . . Dad can go all day swinging the scythe at that pace. He amazes me. I hope I get some muscles this summer so I can do more.

Once Dad has all the grain cut, the next task is to bind the cut sheaves of grain into a sheaf. I think we will be helping him. Since the weather has been so funny and uncertain, he will want it in bundles and off the ground to dry as soon as possible. Dad taught us all how to make sheaves and bundles this way. He grabs with his left hand a handful of the cut grain just below the heads. With his right he grips a bit of the straw and swings it over the heads of grain. Using a straw sticking out, he ties the bundle, making a sheaf. Those sheaves Dad stacks together into a shock with the heads up to dry in a group. Once dry in two to three days when the weather doesn't threaten rain, Dad uses the wagon cover that Barry returned after fixing his roof and places the cover in the middle of the stubble field that has just been cut so he is able to carry the bundles to this area easily. That wagon cover gets its uses! The canvas wagon cover now becomes a threshing floor for the grain sheaves. Using a fork he and Albert recently made, Dad carries the dried sheaves to the "threshing floor," flailing two bundles at a time, continuing to flail until the heads on the top of each straw appear light and empty. Once one side looks empty, Dad turns the bundle over and whales at the sheaves again!

When he feels the sheaves are as empty of grain as he can get them, the grain is sacked and hauled to the bin Dad built in the corner of the stable, using six foot planks. Dad builds the "wall" as high as is needed, adding as many planks as he needs to hold the grain in the make-shift bin. Because of the size of the field, Dad figures it will take us three days to flail the oats, hauling grain sacks home to the bin. That means that the wagon cover will have to be picked up each night and put back each morning so that it doesn't get damp from the dew or wet from rain. Last, Dad uses the schooner (wagon) to haul the straw left from the flailing and brings it home. The straw will be eaten by the cattle in winter if we run out of better feed. Mostly, we use this straw for bedding of the animals in their pens and barn stalls. When I asked Dad what the yield was for this year's crop, Dad said he got only 20 bushels an acre. From the talk at the mill and McConkey's, that is about average yield for those who planted oats in this area this year. The early spring was dry and probably stunted the oats' growth.

John Grantham, a neighbor who lives on a forty west of us, stopped by to talk to Dad about buying a rake. Grantham told Dad that he has a new job. He starts July 31 as an attendant at the insane asylum in Fergus. The hospital has been recently updated, improving living conditions and care for the patients. The patients expected aren't the real loonies and will be treated not like criminals but people who are brain sick. Grantham said the people confined are expected to work around the institution but will also have to play games and do exercises requiring lots of energy. The first group of patients numbering eighty came last Wednesday by train from the St. Peter asylum, he said. Others are due in shortly. The train car, hauled by Great Northern, came as close to the doors as possible before the group was allowed out. A room was assigned each lunatic, and each was expected to work on the grounds at a specific task the following morning. Grantham hopes he will be able to work in the games and exercise area. He is a good ball player and has played on the town baseball team for five years or more, I think. Horseshoes is another favorite game of his. He was fun to listen to. I hope he comes by more often not only to buy items from Dad but just to talk.

When I got up this morning, I knew someone was sick. Mom was packing her "medicine" basket as we like to call it. Sure enough she was off on another "neighborly mission." Mrs. Thomas, whom she often takes with her on these missions, and Mom went to visit the Nimrods today. The family has measles, including Mr. Nimrod. Sara (mother of the Nimrods) has her hands full with the whole family sick, so Mom brought a large meat pie for the family.

Both Mrs. Thomas, her family members and Mom have had measles. So have the rest of us including Murphy, so neither Mrs. Thomas nor Mom were too worried about catching it again. Mrs. Thomas had bread and some medicine that she got at McConkey's store to help dry the sores. While they were there, they helped clean vegetables for a soup and made a pie for the family from the fruit Mrs. Nimrod had available. Mom and Mrs. Thomas took our cutter and paint horse, Benji. Mom knew they would be late coming home and Dad worries less when they have the horse and cart. If they should get lost, our horse will always get them home, because he knows that we always give him an extra bagful of oats once he's back in his stall.

While Mom was gone, Dad and I started harvesting wheat, getting 16 - 18 bushels an acre, a better yield than most have according to the "news" at the mill. The wheat glumes hold the kernels better than the oats glumes do, so Dad didn't have to worry so about shelling out the grain as we handled the sheaves. We set larger shocks of wheat – three pairs of bundles in a row and two bundles on each side, ten to a shock. I helped carry as much as I could. I also went back home for food and water when it was time to eat. The flailing and hauling process was the same as he did with the oats, once again using that wagon cover as the threshing floor. In another corner of the stable, Dad built another bin opposite the first to store some sacked wheat to grind for our own use at the mill.

When we were totally done harvesting the oats and wheat and it was not "heating" anymore from the drying, we covered each of the bins with hay and weighted the hay down with wood lengths so that the chickens and other animals would not spoil the grain. We have to be careful to let the grain dry. It's a funny thing but grain, no matter what kind – wheat, oats, corn, rye – gives off heat as it dries. The grain can get hot enough to start on fire. Thomas paid Dad 20 cents a bushel for what wheat he decided to sell. There was a wagon train going to Perham to sell wheat that Dad could have joined if he wanted. Many farmers decided to move their grain there because of the difference in price they would receive. Perham offered $1.50 per bushel! That's a wonderful price but . . . The trip was a two day trip – meaning carrying food, sleeping out, putting the canvas back on the wagon again, and being dependent on no rain *and* waiting in line with the other farmers for "your turn" to have the grain unloaded. Dad decided he could make more money staying home and filling some of the furniture and equipment orders he has, making up the difference that way in what he would get for the grain in Perham. Mom is so glad. For some reason, there are a few strangers that seem to be roaming around lately. She is more comfortable when Dad is close at hand. I've hung around more lately too for that same reason. Not that I am scared of the strangers – I stay away from them – but I worry too about Mom, Nise and Murphy when they are alone.

When I got up this morning, I looked out the back, hoping I'd see a turkey or two roosting in our trees. I know they are in the area. I have seen one or two fly when I have been out in the woods or walking to the mill. As I looked out, I saw Mr. Grantham coming down the road. He came over today before he went to Fergus to work. This time he didn't need another rake or something else made by Dad but was looking for a horse he had in his barn in a back stall. Seems when he got up this morning to ride it to Fergus, he discovered it was missing. Dad told him we hadn't seen it and looked at me to ask if I had seen it. I shook my head "no."

I went to the mill later to deliver some meals for Mom. Mr. Thomas saw me and asked if we were missing anything at our place. I told him I didn't think so but that Mr. Grantham had lost a horse. Mrs. Thomas' cutter was missing from their place. So was another horse of theirs. Thomas is going to tell the sheriff. The poundmaster has

141

been warned also to be "on the look out" for the men who were around McCarthy's and the Cheese House two days ago. I came home and told Dad that I was staying out of the woods for a while, hoping these guys would move on.

When I walk inside the house, especially after I have been to the Mill or McConkey's for something, Mom usually sits me down and gives me a treat. Nise comes around too. They both are so busy that they rarely get out and about. They are glad to hear the news I bring home, good or bad. It keeps them up to date on what is going on in the area.

Chapter

26

Fall Approaches

August 14th is the earliest most people around here remember harvesting the "late" crops, like potatoes. Dad is glad that he is done harvesting. The oats was not a good crop this year. The wheat was a much better yielding crop. Our potatoes are pretty small in size too for the kind we planted, probably because we did not get the rain we needed in early May.

Today, Dad and I went to Clitherall, the other side of Battle Lake, to get more chickens for Mom's coop! She uses many eggs in her making food for those lunch pails and often runs out. Fletcher, a man who used to live in the Southern part of the state where Grandpa lives that Dad met when we were staying there, wrote a letter stating he had moved to Clitherall and had a black and white speckled rooster with some shiny golden red feathers about the neck and tail along with six hens of various colors: a solid black, one reddish buff, and the others mixed colors. Fletcher's letter stated that the combs and wattles were one color, blood red, which means they are in good health. Fletcher and his family have been raising chickens as long as Grandpa can remember. Mom gave Dad $2.00 from her lunch money box to pay for the seven chickens. We took the crate that the first chickens were shipped in from Fergus Falls last fall on the stage coach with us to confine them in the box that Dad made on the back of the cart for hauling small items. I've never seen such blood red wattles on chickens as those are.

Dad stopped at Clitherall store on the way home out of curiosity, I think. He bought a well-made chopper's axe and chopper mittens that the Indians in the area make. The mitts he has are pretty worn from all the wood that he has cut since we came to this area. Also, we got another wooden pail with iron hoops and several uncommonly large-diameter candles to read by at night.

We hadn't gone far returning home when we ran into two Chippewa Indians standing on the road. Neither Dad nor I speak their language and they did not speak ours, so we did the best we could with sign language. They wanted the single shot gun that we had with us and the ammunition along with it. One had in his arms a great heap of animal pelts that he wanted to barter for the single shot. In the other he had a fine tomahawk and peace pipe. Somehow Dad made them understand that he could not part with the weapon because it kept his family in meat. The two ran off into the woods and we continued on our way. I was shaking when it was all over. We don't see many Indians in the area, so when we do, I get really frightened. When they come around, we try to be as friendly as we can, helping them in whatever way we can. They must sense that we mean no harm to them because they don't bother us when trouble stirs them up. Other farmers immediately chase them off when they see them.

144

We don't do this. Mom usually feeds them whatever she has on hand and then they go on their way again. Most surprising to me was that these two we ran into didn't seem to want the chickens. I thought at first they maybe wanted the rooster for his pretty plume feathers. Maybe they didn't see him in the crate. It was a terribly noisy ride once we got going again with all the squawking going on behind us from the confined flock as we traveled down the bumpy road home. I would have liked to sleep but that was impossible with the awful noise.

Ross stopped today, wanting to see the new colored chickens and rooster he knew we picked up yesterday. He had been to the mill and heard the men talking as they waited in line to grind grain. Did he have a story to tell me! Seems like the Kysors have had more trouble. George's (Mr. Kysor) team became frightened while working in the field hooked to a binder and ran away with Kysor still on the binder. The binder broke, piling George and the two horses in a heap. The binder is a loss but Kysor and the horses are sore but fine. Kysor's threshing crew saw the accident and was able to help the horses and him unwind from the wreck. Pretty scary! A tumble with the equipment can wreck a man's life, being hurt like that!

Ross also told me that Thomas is adding a sloping roof to the mill. Early August has meant 20 to 30 wagons, each with about 20 sacks of grain, stretching from one end of Maine to the other and sometimes beyond. The mill can run 60 – 70 barrels a day, producing Patent, Straight, Bakers and low grade flours. Ezra Adams is Thomas' partner and my good friend. Ezra works long hours and is known as the best miller in the area. Sometimes when I bring a meal to the waiting farmers, I bring Ezra lunch too. I think that is why Ezra shuts his eyes when he sees me fishing by the mill wheel, where I am not supposed to be. I also help sew bags shut when I can. I like those copper pennies I earn when I sew and usually spend them at McConkey's store. Sometimes I go to the cheese house instead and surprise Mom with a slice when I have enough cash in my pocket. I love cheese. I have grown up eating it as long as I can remember.

Anton came with his dad yesterday and told me that the grain they brought to grind made 12 sacks of Gold Foil Patent that would sell for $28.20, four ½ sacks of Silver Leaf Fancy for $17.20, twelve ¼ sacks of Graham for $5.40, and two and ½ sacks Bakers Choice for $3.80. Anton is from Pelican Rapids. He and his dad bring grain to be ground from farmers there, who each order their grain ground a certain way. When Anton is here, we always go down to the dam. Pelican has a dam too and we compare "notes." It sounds like there are more fish that hang around the Pelican dam, probably because there isn't a mill. Kids use the one side of the Pelican dam as a swimming pond, jumping in from the bridge across. I want to go see it. Maybe Dad will take me soon. After we had nosed around our mill here in Maine, Anton and I went down to the Roost to see the horses in the stalls and to wait for his dad to get done. Frank, who manages the Roost, handed me the papers that had been left by the men who had their horses and mules there while they waited for the grain to be ground. A new area newspaper was in the batch.

Wheelock is printing a *Weekly* newspaper in competition with the *Fergus Falls Weekly*. The Wheelock paper I got at the Roost was the September 11th issue. Hubbard had an advertisement in the paper, wanting to buy milk. Hubbard is our good cheese maker and needs 700 pounds of milk a day. Ten pounds of milk makes one pound of cheese. Farmers that had milk cans full were in a long line by the Cheese House yesterday waiting to unload and now I know why. That advertisement must have brought them. Hubbard gives the farmers a choice of cash for the milk or cheese in trade. Reports are that the cheese factory is doing a "rushing business," averaging 1500 pounds of milk daily, way over the limit of 700 that

Hubbard hoped for when he built this spring. There is always activity around there these days.

The Barry boys are building an ice house, using the family's old sod house. The old soddy on the homestead where they live hasn't been used in four years and is starting to come apart. The boys decided to cut ice this winter and store it to sell to the area people including the Cheese House and McConkey's store. First task was to repair the roof, adding sod in places where it had blown or washed away. Two of the boys were on one side of the roof repairing; two were on the other side. The rest of the Barry boys lugged the heavier sod cuttings, handing them up to whichever pair needed them. I helped for a while. The thin ones usually used on a roof would not be thick enough to control keeping in the cold and keeping out the heat of summer so they were using the thicker sod blocks only. The good thing about being from a large family is that "many hands make quick work" or whatever that saying is.

Once the roof was done, it was time to shore up the walls with sod and boards. Boards were attached across horizontally to the end poles to help hold the walls more securely in place. Next, the boys took straw and built up along the inside walls to make them thicker in order to hold the cold in and the heat of summer out. Two of the boys drove the cart back and forth from the field where the straw from the wheat they harvested lay. The others carried in the straw by armfuls, laying it along the inside of the walls. Even the windows were covered with sod, tar paper and straw.

Once the walls were reinforced to control the temperature, they had to repair the door which had blown off its hinges in one of the summer windstorms. McConkey had a new hinge so that turned out to be the easiest task.

Finishing the house, the plan of the Barry boys was to make the rounds of all the close neighbors and store owners to see how many would be interested in having ice blocks delivered every three days starting early in January when they could get on the lake to cut blocks, continuing through spring and summer until their supply of cut ice blocks is gone or melts. The blocks would be 5 cents each. They also talked about going to the Maine north of here and doing the same thing there. The boys will need saw dust to pack the ice blocks in, but that should not be a problem with all the wood cutting that goes on around here. It will be interesting to see how many people take up the offer and how long the boys get along well enough to work together. Most of the time, they are squabbling between themselves, not wanting to help each other. At least it seems that way during recess at school. Boy, can they fight! Those brothers fight amongst themselves but stick together against outsiders when the family reputation is threatened!

Chapter

28

Preparing for Winter

We have a new teacher again in District 22. The school board met September 4th and hired L. G. Perry from Iowa to teach this year. Mr. Perry taught a term here last year, when J. Gaylord suddenly left. The sheriff where Gaylord came from finally caught up with him. In order to get here this spring, Mr. Gaylord took his neighbor's horse without asking, intending to return it at the end of the school year. He forgot to write a letter to his neighbor, explaining what he had done. The sheriff from there had a warrant for his arrest and he was taken by stage back to his home in Iowa to answer the charge - something about a bad horse trade, I think is how the warrant read. Some states hang people for horse stealing! Even if he is forgiven by the neighbor, the school board did not think he was a good character model for the school. I hope Gaylord can work something out with the law in Iowa. I don't think he took the horse intentionally, but I do not know that for sure.

As far as teachers go, I like Mr. Perry better. He is a good science teacher and a wonderful artist. He helped me get the perspective of my drawings right. I used to make table legs too short for the top. He showed me a simple way to judge, using the edges of the paper, to tell what the length of each leg and the other objects I am drawing should be according to where they are placed in the drawing. Mr. Perry is much younger than Gaylord was and comes out to play baseball with us during our noon recess. Once last year, he hit the ball so hard that it flew and broke one of the schoolhouse windows. He felt really bad about it, especially because he had to report it to the school board *and* pay for the repair.

After the school board recently met September 8th at school, Perry Kysor and the crew that he hires to thresh with his threshing machine held their meeting there the same night. All joined the Knights of Labor when the Knights Lodge met. Townspeople were surprised that the Knights let the crew join. Kysor's crew does not believe in just working an eight hour day like the Knights expect their members to do. Perry and his crew worked right up to the "front edge" of Sunday last week to get Barry's crop off his land before rain came again. The crew threshed out 17 acres of wheat after dark, absolutely against the Knights of Labor rules! Working that close to Sunday is also against Knights rules. Other "news" was being passed around at the mill this morning when I was there and I really wanted to stay and listen, but I thought I should get going so I could pick the onions for Mom that I found as I came home from school yesterday. I always keep a lookout for fresh food like these onions I saw. Fresh food, no matter what it is, is always a treat for us.

Mom used some of the wild onions today that I picked. Was she ever happy to get them! Mom made Wild

Onions with Apples to go with a goose Dad shot. The onions are fried in oil and added to cooked apples that she peels, cores and cuts into quarters. Steaming tenderizes the apples and blends the two flavors, making a nice meat sauce for coon or geese. Usually she cans the saucy mixture so that we have it on hand when we need it to "cover" the "game taste" of some meat, especially an animal that is older that has been shot.

I can tell it is fall. It's time to store up! Nise and I went out picking nuts today. We both like the spiced nut nibble Mom makes and stores until winter when we sit by the fire and read or play games as a family. She has to buy pecans from the store but we are able to pick walnuts, hazelnuts, and hickory nuts for the mix. It's a little early to pick them. If we don't get going, the squirrels will start stashing them and none will be left for us. I can tell that the bears have already been at the hazelnuts from the sign around the trees. The allspice, cloves, ginger, nutmeg, salt and cinnamon Mom uses in the egg white that she beats and dips the nuts in makes them so tasty once they have been baked a while. Usually we complain when we are sent out to pick, especially this time of year because the mosquitoes are so bad when it is not windy. Nut picking is another story. Both of us go with smiles on our faces, knowing what a treat these nuts will be come winter.

Hubbard had to close his cheese factory until next spring. Winter dry up of the cows in the area has slowed the milk being brought to process into cheese. There are still a few cows that are having calves this time of year but the farmers tend to keep the milk, etc., to use or sell to those who don't have any. With so little milk available, it isn't worth Hubbard's time to fix a single batch of cheese each day. He has bulk cheese packed in ice and sawdust stored in a shed on one side of the sod house. He will sell to customers as long as the cheese holds out. When he started this spring, he did not think he would get enough milk in to have cheese left to sell in September, expecting

151

the dry up season would start about then. I guess there are more cows in this area than we all think. Since his wife can handle the sales of cheese, Hubbard is helping out some of the farmers that are finishing threshing. Most farmers in the area think they will be done around Oct. 1st and that the average yield will run about 16 bushel per acre for the wheat.

While the men are trying to finish the harvest, most women in the area are dealing with their gardens. Mom is really busy now. We had our first frost and that means all the vegetables have to come out of the garden. Today we dug all the potatoes, beets, rutabagas, and carrots. When we could, we used a fork to help lift the vegetables so we could put them in the wicker baskets to lug them over to the horse cart, removing as much of the dirt as possible. When we got a cart load full, we brought the vegetables to the root cellar. The turnips, rutabagas and carrots we took down and covered with sand dug from the hill outside and moistened with river water. The potatoes we dug we put outside by the house on a canvas to dry in the sun so we could rub the dried dirt off and store in the cellar. Onions were dried in the sun too but taken to the barn and buried in a stanchion filled with hay.

Dad made a cellar hole before he began building the house that has an escape hatch to the outside. Grandpa John told Dad to be prepared for the storms that can come in this area, mostly wind storms, and the two of them designed this 8 x 8 foot cellar under the house, a little larger than was first planned. The walls are of rock picked when we first cleared the land. Dad sloped the rocks eight inches or more across one on top of the other and the weight of each one holds a wall in place. The trap door in the house is in the wash room where we wash before meals, built into the floor. Mom can lift the trap door, go down the ladder made from poplar that leans on the wall below and get any vegetables she wants. She stores her canned meat, fruit, and vegetables down there too. I steal pickles from the pickle crock each time I get a chance to go down there.

Chapter

29

Parties and Pranks

I went this morning to see where Thomas and Adams built another good shed to better stable the horses of the farmers waiting to grind grain. The first shed was a lean-to affair, not insulated very well and not very big. The new shed can hold 16 good sized horses the size of Logan, the Clydesdale owned by Fred Hanson who brings him here and hires him out each year for sire. The new stable will be much warmer and more comfortable for teams that stay over night. This October weather is so unpredictable. It will be good for the animals to have an enclosed area away from the cold rain and wind we get at this time of year.

Town has been busy with events like Logan coming again to "stand at stud" and so many landowners bringing their grain for grinding. I love Logan! I sneak a carrot with me from our root cellar every time that I know he will be in town. When I come in, Logan snorts and shakes his head up and down, just like he is greeting me. The carrot is gone in one bite. I spend time talking to him when I can. He is so big but I feel so protected by him even if he towers over me. It's hard for me to leave him and finish the rest of my lunch deliveries.

The mill is buzzing with people all excited about one thing. Thomas is talking about renaming the mill after his wife's family, the **Phelps**. The stagecoach and others who come to town with shipments get so confused with the two Maine towns, ours and the one just north of here where the other school and our church is. Mail is confusing too. If our Maine is renamed, I suppose our town will become **Phelps** and the mill **Phelps Mill**.

Usually by Halloween, which was last night, the mill has slowed down some. Last week I heard Thomas say that they have all the work his mill can do during the day times. It has been so busy that he ran the mill some nights last week when the moon was full and the weather was warm and nice, in order to catch up.

The Anderson boys were at it again Halloween night. One of the boys dressed up as the headless horseman, much like the horseman in the "Legend of Sleepy Hollow" story that Mr. Perry read to us at school. The only difference is that that horseman is very tall and big boned in the story. One of Reverend Anderson's son's is short and pretty pudgy. He rode a horse and had a pumpkin under his arm just like we read. The younger son, Francis, ran ahead of him, dressed in a black cape and yelled, "Beware! Beware! He comes! He comes!" Their Dad discovered they were gone and followed them in to town last night. I am sure that the hickory stick got used when he finally got those boys home! Pastor believes in "spare the rod and spoil the child!"

I think to make up for the fuss that his sons caused Halloween night, the minister and his wife are having another "Whosoever Will" social November 12th and this

155

time they are roasting one of Beckford's Poland Chinas. Mr. Beckford is proud of his pigs and donated one for the social if the Andersons would fix it. Everyone is to come, bringing a dish to share, picnic style. I am sure we won't be dancing, nor will there be any drinking. Party games will be played after the furniture is pushed to the side of the room.

My favorite party game is "Hunt the Thimble." I like to hide the thimble when the others are out of the room or hide their eyes so they don't see what I am doing. I try and hide it very low, beside a chair leg. Most of us look up, missing what is on the floor. The other game we play gets very noisy. It is "Button, Button." Whoever starts the game walks around the circle, pretending to place the button in each person's hand, finally leaving it in one of the player's hand. It is important to continue walking after the button has been put in someone's hand so that the group does not suspect it has been dropped in a hand. Once the "dropper" sits, the people in the group start to shout the name of the person he or she thinks has the button. Whoever guesses the right person is next to drop the button and the guessing continues. I get bored playing this game. Most just call out names, hoping to call the right name and be the "dropper." It is more interesting to watch Neil, Ross' brother, and Nise make eyes at each other across the circle. If it weren't for the parties, they would not be able to see very much of each other.

We came home late last night after the "Whosoever Will" so Mom let us kids sleep late. Am I glad or I would have had to help Dad. He came in stinking today after working in the barn. He took chunks of stable manure and smeared the chinks in the stable walls with it to defend against the winter blasts. McConkey's store was out of the other hole patching material we used on the house, and McConkey did not know when the next batch would come by stage so Dad used the next best thing. Mom made him strip his clothes off at the door, put them in the laundry basket and leave them outside until he went to the barn again where they will be stored until she has a chance to wash clothes. It is colder now so she doesn't wash as often. He washed as best he could in the sideboard sink since it is now too cold to go take a bath in the river or lake.

It's a good thing we just made the two-day trip to Fergus Falls last week to shop for clothes, or Dad would have been hard up to find a good pair of overalls. Most of his overalls, including the one he had on to chink the stable walls, have holes in the knees. We stayed in one of the hotels overnight. What a treat! Nise, Murphy and I had one room and Mom and Dad had the room next door. Our rooms included beef stew, bread and pie for supper and a huge farmer's breakfast of oatmeal, pancakes, fried potatoes, and bacon. The bathroom was down the hall inside! That was a treat too! Usually we have to go outside to the outhouse, no matter how cold or dark it is. Unless we are sick, the chamber pot stays under our bed or we have to clean it in the morning. That's Mom's rule.

Chapter

30

Hunting Season

It's November 14th and Dad's birthday. Mom made him his favorite cake, an angel food, whipped some cream and had strawberry syrup to pour on. He was all smiles when we celebrated after supper. These short days of November and the long nights find Dad and I building a monstrous sledge for hauling wood during the winter *and* another harrow. The harrow we have is well used due to those rocks that we continue to dodge in the fields.

Dad needs to get more lumber ready before the snow flies. He gets orders to build various tools, furniture and farm equipment. Dad is paid good money for what he builds because he is so particular about making sure any item will withstand a hard use. If the orders continue and his reputation as a carpenter grows, he says he will hire out the land on shares, spending his time in the wood shop. Maybe I will get to try farrowing this spring. I have sure grown but I am not sure I have the strength yet for it. Seems like I am either too small to do some things, too young to do others or not strong enough. Even hunting is sometimes hard for me when I have to deal with a heavy carcass. Once or twice, I have had to cut the deer up and bring it home in sections.

Deer hunting season starts November 27th, next weekend. The season is late this year but the hunters are all happy. Tracking is much easier when there is snow on the ground like we have now. Wes White and Clay Burns from our church went up into St. Louis County near Aitkin to hunt. Going that far with a horse and sleigh seems dumb to me when we have the deer population that we have around here. Dad and I went out to set our deer stand up in a tree, just a board up in a comfortable crook in the tree. We will be up early next Saturday, before daybreak so we can get to the stand at daylight. It's my first real hunt and I can't wait. I hope I see Ross tomorrow at the mill so I can tell him about the stand.

We had to put off deer hunting a day because Dad needed to see Albert about a harrow the two are making. When we went by the mill, we heard Mosher announce to all the farmers that he and his son are buying hogs, sheep and veal calves. He was offering 10 cents a pound more than is paid either in Battle Lake or Fergus. Beckford, who raises pigs, sold off his Chester Whites and half of his Poland Chinas to Mosher. While I was talking to Ross, Dad heard that Mosher will ship them to St. Paul on the train. Won't that be a noisy stinky mess!

Mosher had Dad build a simple log barn from flat logs last week. The barn is to be used as a sort of corral for the animals as they wait to be put on the train and shipped out. Sure enough! When I came down to deliver some lunches Thomas said a carload was shipped yesterday when the train stopped near here on his property. Mosher intends to ship another load next Monday.

159

This area is just hopping with business of one kind or another. One of those businesses is the pig farm. H. Epler moved from Otter Tail, a town northeast of here December 6th and hired out a soddy and large barn out east of town. Next, he bought a full blooded Poland China boar from Beckford to be the sire for his passel of pigs that he moved with him. Beckford's Poles are reportedly the best in the area. Epler's farm is quite the operation, according to Beckford. Some people call this kind of an operation a "pig mill." They say that all Epler does is breed and raise, breed and raise – not worrying about the health of the animal. I don't like that kind of use of an animal. Dad has always taught me to treat animals like I would treat a human. I don't know any women that are pregnant all the time so I don't see why a pig should be either.

I remember Grandpa John telling us when we stayed with them last year about buying his first pigs one time from his neighbor when he first came here from Norway and homesteaded. Grandpa got the three sows into a cart and started down the road towards home. A wolf jumped out of the woods and scared Grandpa's horse, making it gallop down the road, shaking the gate in the back of the cart open. Out tumbled the pigs and into the woods they went. It took him two hours of scrambling over downed wood and through the trees to catch the pigs again and get them back in the cart. Grandpa still laughs so hard telling the story now, but I bet he was mad when it happened.

While I was waiting for Dad to get done talking to Albert about the harrow, I watched Harry out behind the Roost. Harry is Harry Pittitt, Dr. Pittitt's son, an "old" school friend of mine who has hunted grouse with me. I miss his quick aim and ability to spot those birds that blend so well into the fall foliage. He is home from medical school, and was working with Mr. Kysor's bronco, trying to break it. He has broken other horses for other people before without getting hurt. This time he wasn't so lucky. The horse

160

reached for Harry with his hind feet, hitting Harry on the leg and in the stomach as he kicked. Kysor brought Harry to Dr. Pittitt's office by carriage. He seems recovered. He's lucky to have a dad as smart as Dr. Pittitt is. Later Harry told me he will board the stagecoach tomorrow when it comes and go back to school, hoping to finish by next spring. He was sorry to leave so soon, missing all the chances to hunt turkey this time of year.

Yesterday I got a chance to go to my first turkey shoot. Jas. Fogard invited anyone interested in a turkey shoot to come out to his farm. Dad reluctantly took me. Most of his reluctance was his having to buy a gun for the shoot. My old twelve guage would have blown the birds apart. I spent the two days before the shoot practicing in the back yard, pretending to aim at the turkey's head.

We took the cutter and horse over to Fogards, picking Ross up on the way. He wanted to come and watch. Turkeys are not necessarily easy to hunt. They roost in trees so they are visible but they fly too. Because they are a heavier bird, you think they can't fly very far and tend to shoot ahead of where they are, thinking they can't fly so fast. It gets frustrating because they usually fly into the trees and under the cover of the leaves. We were told that the shoot was easier this year because of all the early snow. We did not have as much trouble tracking and shooting the birds because the leaves were gone. The limit was three each.

The Nygren boys took the most turkeys home, each shot one or more. Dad and I got one large tom. He will be good for Christmas Dinner. Dad cleaned him when we got home and put him in the smokehouse to cure until then.

When we were done with the hunt, the Fogards set up targets. They had a prize for the best shot out of ten targets at 30 yards. I let Ross use my gun to try to get the prize. Since he hadn't ever shot it, he hit one out of the ten, not very good. Some fellow from Pelican won. I guess he is a regular at the turkey shoots around here and often wins any target shooting.

Some of the men at the shoot were talking about the ruckus the women have caused at church. Yes, the church women are at it again! Usually it is the Temperance Meeting that stirs the fuss. Not this time! The scheme afoot that the men gossiped about is to build sheds for the horses at the church in the other town of Maine where the church is. The women have raised forty dollars already, and more money is expected in soon. Women have ways of wheedling money out of their men. They are also planning an auction just before Christmas now, hoping to sweeten the pot and get the barn built before the cold of January sets in.

We see Indians once in a while in this area. The last time I saw one was when Dad and I were hunting ducks on the Red in October. Two were across the river in a canoe, paddling up the Red towards Fergus. We have no idea why they were around. The December 18th's *Weekly* announced Sitting Bull's death. He was at the Standing Rock Reservation, I think. The story talks about a Ghost Dance Religion which sounds much like our church gatherings. They were going to dance, hoping the messiah would come. We go to church, praying we are ready when Jesus next comes. I can't see much difference in the ideas except that Reverend Anderson does not dance around like the Indians do when he talks about Jesus' coming again. The Bureau of Indian Affairs told the Indians that they couldn't dance - that dancing wasn't religious. This made the Indians mad. The Bureau arrested Sitting Bull in hopes of stopping the rumbling. It didn't work. The warriors gathered and tried to rescue Sitting Bull. Somehow, Sitting Bull was killed in the fight. Seems like a pretty silly thing to fight over, this Ghost Dancing. What would it hurt? All kinds of other religions in the area, like the one Maria Blaisdell once started in

Pelican, meet regularly. Nobody tells them what they can and cannot do to worship.

Good thing there is other activity around the mill to keep people's minds off the Indian affairs. Thomas is building again and has his sheds up and enclosed, but work still needs to be done to get the sheds ready for the teams. There continue to be so many people coming each day to grind grain and Thomas feels he needs to provide shelter for them, especially now that it is getting colder. Thomas put out a call to the farmers in the area who have extra time now that the fieldwork is done to come and help. He is offering reduced cost to grind grain if someone helps with the barn.

The extra people around means someone needs to feed them. Mom is kept as busy as she wants to be. It's harder for her to keep meals that she sells to the farmers at the mill hot now that the weather has changed. She takes the pails packed with food and puts them in that new wood pail with a wood cover that Dad and I bought in Clitherall, surrounding each pail inside the bucket with small wool blanket wraps or baked potatoes that help insolate against the cold. I sell the potatoes too. If I run fast, the food is still warm and the farmers give Mom and me both a tip.

When I got home from my last "mill" run, Mom was really unhappy. Seems one of our prize colored roosters is gone. This is the first time we have ever had anything stolen on the homestead. I asked Mom if she thought it might have been a weasel. She didn't know what had happened, only that the rooster was gone. The more I thought about it being a weasel, the more I realized that a weasel would have "wiped out" all of the critters in the coop, not just a rooster. To take Mom's mind off the loss, I stuck around and told her all the "news" I had heard from town.

I told Mom that people at the mill and at McConkey's store were talking about the chicken thieves active in the area. Most wonder if it can be blamed to the Anderson

163

boys again! The thieves have been warned by an announcement hanging at the mill and at McConkey's store. Pepper shot is usually used to discourage unwanted predators, man or animal. The last few December nights have been warmer than usual, tempting people to do mischief. Nice weather tends to mean people with time on their hands get into trouble. The minister's sons don't have many chores to do like the rest of us, so it is possible they have found a new way to keep "busy."

Many wonder if there will be enough snow for Christmas this year so we can use the sleighs. We have had few mornings with fresh snow on the ground. No snow makes walking to school easier. We don't get as wet from the drifts higher than our shoe tops that get inside our shoes. Because of the lack of snow, Murphy hasn't been as sick as he has been other years at this time. Usually, when he gets wet being outside, his tonsils get so sore that he spends two or three days in front of the stove getting better. If we don't get more snow, we won't be able to go visit Grandpa and Grandma. We haven't been together with them for Christmas since we moved here so Mom and Dad plan to go this year. Most cutters are too small for a family to use to visit any distance. We really can't take the schooner or wagon and risk getting stuck with it if we do have a good snowfall. As much as I want to visit them, I sure don't want to have to spend a night stuck in a snowbank in the schooner. That would be cold!

The Barry boys hope that the weather doesn't get too warm. They are anxious to start cutting ice blocks to store for their new business venture. I suppose it will be mid January before they really get going. It usually takes that long for the ice to thicken enough to have a decent block.

Chapter

31

Year's End

J. Morton and Co. opened a new store close to the mill today. I haven't been in but I have watched them from the mill as they moved merchandise into the building. I know the Barrys have an ice order for them as soon as they can cut blocks. I hope Nise can find work there. She is tired of working around home and too young to apply for a teaching certificate yet. She is still going to school, but Mr. Perry's teaching certificate is not issued for her grade. Mom, Dad, and Mr. Perry are all trying to help her so she can pass the county test when it is given to become a teacher herself.

Anton and his dad came from Pelican again to grind grain. Anton was here with his dad in October and he and I fished off the shore of Lake Leon, catching some nice bass last time he was here. Anton came running to the house to get me and said he had a surprise for me. We ran back to the mill and, sure enough, on top of the sacks of grain was a spruce tree for our house. I had complained the last time he was here that we did not have any big trees suitable for a Christmas tree. Most of our trees were oak, basswood, poplar, etc. He remembered and brought one for us. The two of us wrestled the tree off the wagon, lugging it over to the road and up to our house. Dad was in the barn and helped Anton and me fashion a base to set it in so we could put the tree up inside. Nise ran to McConkeys and got colored paper. When she got back, the three of us made daisy chains, using flour paste to fasten the ends of the paper, linking each to make a chain. Mom popped a batch of popcorn and we sewed the popped kernels together in another chain. We worked all afternoon. Anton enjoyed helping. In fact, he stayed overnight with us because the mill was so busy that Anton's dad could not get his grain ground until morning.

This first Christmas in the log house will be a special memory for me, I know, now that we have a spruce tree in our house. Mom went to her knitting stash and gave Anton a pair of mittens for his dad and him as he left this morning. He at first refused but finally took them. His mittens had holes in them and it is a long ride back to Pelican for the two of them. I know he will be glad he said yes when they get on the road.

It's hard to believe that we have been here as long as we have. I remember that we celebrated Murphy's 5th birthday, the first day we were on our land. I have some thinking to do in the next few days. Mr. McConkey offered me a job in his store. If I take this job, two things happen. First, I have to move in with the McConkeys so I am available all the time to run errands when the stage comes in, deliver supplies, or deliver mail and messages. I will also stock shelves and package some of the stock into smaller quantities for him. Second, I will have to quit school. He wants me to start working for him when the New Year begins and that is only three days away.

Working for Mr McConkey will be easy. I am not sure quitting school is what I want to do. Mom and Dad have left the decision up to me. Dad has decided to hire out the land and just do carpentry work. Nise can run the meals to the mill, I guess. That leaves me free to decide. Problem is I have dreamed about becoming a printer apprentice in a newspaper shop. If I do this, I will have to move to Fergus or another town where there is a newspaper *and* a printer willing to teach me how to set and run a printing press. I have heard that the new *Weekly* just started in Fergus needs help. With my love for books, this is a real dream job for me. I don't even think it would be work as most people think of work.

I don't really mind farming in the way that Dad farms either. I don't especially like working with the animals but I like the crop raising part. I know that may seem strange since I complain so much about weeding the garden. But weeding the crops or planting hasn't seemed like work to me ever. Threshing is dusty and dirty but so is most work, no mater whether it is inside work or outside work. One thing is for certain. I am not a carpenter. I don't have the patience to spend the time finishing a project like Dad does. I can put things together but I hate sanding, and re-sanding to give that special finish.

Sleep the last two nights hasn't come easily. I've had much on my mind. I have made a decision and told Mom and Dad this morning when I got up and we were eating breakfast. I decided to move over to McConkey's tomorrow and get ready to go to work. I had tears in my eyes and so did Mom. I know in my heart that if I do not like working there, I can always try finding an apprenticeship with a printer. Then too, Dad has hired out the land for the next year. Even if I wanted to start with the crops, I could not this year anyway. This will give me some time to decide what I want to do. I told them I would try working with McConkey until school starts next fall. If it

167

works out well, I won't go back to school. I know I can catch up the time I missed if I decide to return to school. Learning comes easily for me. I went the bedroom and started packing my things in a box Mom gave me. Murphy doesn't know what to think. He asks if I am moving out to the fort. I try to explain. Nise even has tears in her eyes. Imagine that! My sister will miss me! Tonight is the end of 1890. Tomorrow is a new venture for me.

Coming Soon

Sequel

Remembering the *Maine* Riding with Roosevelt

Remembering the *Maine* continues the story of young Nivek James. Leaving his family homestead in Minnesota, he becomes a newspaper correspondent during the Spanish-American War. Together with his boyhood friends, Wing, an Ojibwa Indian, and Jesse, from Medora, North Dakota, the young men travel across country by horseback, train, and stagecoach on their journey to join the Rough Riders and Theodore Roosevelt. This book is the story of their journey, the training of the troops, and the war in Cuba. It is a coming-of-age tale of bravery, courage, hardships and patriotism set against the background of the emergence of the U.S.A. as a world power. Nivek's dispatches to the **Minnesota News** give a personal account of the times.

Jan Smith writes Historical Fiction in the classical style. Taking documented incidents in the lives and times of well known individuals during the period of the Spanish American War, Smith intersperses other characters and events in order to make the story enjoyable reading.

Made in the USA
Charleston, SC
21 May 2013